PREVIOUS PRAISE FOR
GEORGE SAUNDERS

"Not since Twain has America produced a satirist this funny." —*Zadie Smith*

"The person I'm highest on right now is George Saunders, whose book *CivilWarLand in Bad Decline* just came out and is well worth a great deal of attention."
—*David Foster Wallace, in Salon*

"[I] read Saunders because he always makes me want to write. He reads like he's having such a good time and I love his humor so much. . . . He was one of those writers he just opened doors and doors for me." —*Karen Russell*

"An astoundingly tuned voice—graceful, dark, authentic, and funny—telling just the kinds of stories we need to get us through these times." —*Thomas Pynchon*

"A multifaceted writer, very easy on the surface to pin down but incredibly difficult once you actually read him with any depth." —*Joshua Ferris, in The New Yorker Book Bench*

"Saunders is a writer of arresting brilliance and originality, with a sure sense of his material and apparently inexhaustible resources of voice. . . . Scary, hilarious, and unforgettable." —*Tobias Wolff*

"George Saunders is so funny and inventive he makes you love words and so wide-eyed wistful he talks you into loving people." —*Sarah Vowell*

Also by George Saunders

FICTION

CivilWarLand in Bad Decline

Pastoralia

The Very Persistent Gappers of Frip

The Brief and Frightening Reign of Phil

In Persuasion Nation

ESSAYS

The Braindead Megaphone

TENTH of DECEMBER

TENTH of DECEMBER

Stories

GEORGE SAUNDERS

RANDOM HOUSE · NEW YORK

Published in the United States by Random House, an imprint of The Random House Publishing Group, a division of Random House, Inc., New York.

RANDOM HOUSE and colophon are registered trademarks of Random House, Inc.

The stories in this work were originally published in *Harper's Magazine, McSweeney's Quarterly Concern, The New Yorker,* and *Story Magazine.*

Library of Congress Cataloging-in-Publication Data
Saunders, George.
Tenth of December : stories / George Saunders.
p. cm.
ISBN 978-0-8129-9380-6
eBook ISBN 978-0-8129-9381-3
I. Title.
PS3569.A7897T46 2013
813'.54—dc23   2012013782

Printed in the United States of America on acid-free paper

www.atrandom.com

2 4 6 8 9 7 5 3 1

First Edition

Book design by Diane Hobbing

For Pat Pacino

CONTENTS

TENTH of DECEMBER

VICTORY LAP

Three days shy of her fifteenth birthday, Alison Pope paused at the top of the stairs.

Say the staircase was marble. Say she descended and all heads turned. Where was {special one}? Approaching now, bowing slightly, he exclaimed, How can so much grace be contained in one small package? Oops. Had he said *small package*? And just stood there? Broad princelike face totally bland of expression? Poor thing! Sorry, no way, down he went, he was definitely not {special one}.

What about this guy, behind Mr. Small Package, standing near the home entertainment center? With a thick neck of farmer integrity yet tender ample lips, who, placing one hand on the small of her back, whispered, Dreadfully sorry you had to endure that bit about the small package just now. Let us go stand on the moon. Or, uh, in the moon. In the moonlight.

Had he said, *Let us go stand on the moon*? If so, she would have to be like, {eyebrows up}. And if no wry acknowledgment was forthcoming, be like, Uh, I am not exactly dressed for standing on the moon, which, as I understand it, is super-cold?

Come on, guys, she couldn't keep treading gracefully on this marble stairwell in her mind forever! That dear old white-hair in the tiara was getting all like, *Why are those supposed princes making that darling girl march in place ad nausea?* Plus she had a recital tonight and had to go fetch her tights from the dryer.

Egads! One found oneself still standing at the top of the stairs.

Do the thing where, facing upstairs, hand on railing, you hop down the stairs one at a time, which was getting a lot harder lately, due to, someone's feet were getting longer every day, seemed like.

Pas de chat, pas de chat.

Changement, changement.

Hop over thin metal thingie separating hallway tile from living-room rug.

Curtsy to self in entryway mirror.

Come on, Mom, get here. We do not wish to be castrigated by Ms. Callow again in the wings.

Although actually she loved Ms. C. So strict! Also loved

the other girls in class. And the girls from school. *Loved* them. Everyone was so nice. Plus the boys at her school. Plus the teachers at her school. All of them were doing their best. Actually, she loved her whole town. That adorable grocer, spraying his lettuce! Pastor Carol, with her large comfortable butt! The chubby postman, gesticulating with his padded envelopes! It had once been a mill town. Wasn't that crazy? What did that even mean?

Also she loved her house. Across the creek was the Russian church. So ethnic! That onion dome had loomed in her window since her Pooh footie days. Also loved Gladsong Drive. Every house on Gladsong was a Corona del Mar. That was amazing! If you had a friend on Gladsong, you already knew where everything was in his or her home.

Jeté, jeté, rond de jambe.

Pas de bourrée.

On a happy whim, do front roll, hop to your feet, kiss the picture of Mom and Dad taken at Penney's back in the Stone Ages, when you were that little cutie right there {kiss} with a hair bow bigger than all outdoors.

Sometimes, feeling happy like this, she imagined a baby deer trembling in the woods.

Where's your mama, little guy?

I don't know, the deer said in the voice of Heather's little sister Becca.

Are you afraid? she asked it. Are you hungry? Do you want me to hold you?

Okay, the baby deer said.

Here came the hunter now, dragging the deer's mother by the antlers. Her guts were completely splayed. Jeez, that was nice! She covered the baby's eyes and was like, Don't you have anything better to do, dank hunter, than kill this baby's mom? You seem like a nice enough guy.

Is my mom killed? the baby said in Becca's voice.

No, no, she said. This gentleman was just leaving.

The hunter, captivated by her beauty, toffed or doffed his cap, and, going down on one knee, said, If I could will life back into this fawn, I would do so, in hopes you might defer one tender kiss upon our elderly forehead.

Go, she said. Only, for your task of penance, do not eat her. Lay her out in a field of clover, with roses strewn about her. And bestow a choir, to softly sing of her foul end.

Lay who out? the baby deer said.

No one, she said. Never mind. Stop asking so many questions.

Pas de chat, pas de chat.

Changement, changement.

She felt hopeful that {special one} would hail from far away. The local boys possessed a certain *je ne sais quoi,* which, tell the truth, she was not *très* crazy about, such as: actually named their own nuts. She had overheard that! And aspired to work for CountyPower because the work shirts were awesome and you got them free.

So ixnay on the local boys. A special ixnay on Matt Drey, owner of the largest mouth in the land. Kissing him last night at the pep rally had been like kissing an underpass.

Scary! Kissing Matt was like suddenly this cow in a sweater is bearing down on you, who will not take no for an answer, and his huge cow head is being flooded by chemicals that are drowning out what little powers of reason Matt actually did have.

What she liked was being in charge of her. Her body, her mind. Her thoughts, her career, her future.

That was what she liked.

So be it.

We might have a slight snack.

Un petit repas.

Was she special? Did she consider herself special? Oh, gosh, she didn't know. In the history of the world, many had been more special than her. Helen Keller had been awesome; Mother Teresa was amazing; Mrs. Roosevelt was quite chipper in spite of her husband, who was handicapped, which, in addition, she had been gay, with those big old teeth, long before such time as being gay and First Lady was even conceptual. She, Alison, could not hope to compete in the category of those ladies. Not yet, anyway!

There was so much she didn't know! Like how to change the oil. Or even check the oil. How to open the hood. How to bake brownies. That was embarrassing, actually, being a girl and all. And what was a mortgage? Did it come with the house? When you breast-fed, did you have to like push the milk out?

Egads. Who was this wan figure, visible through the living-room window, trotting up Gladsong Drive? Kyle Boot, palest kid in all the land? Still dressed in his weird cross-country toggles?

Poor thing. He looked like a skeleton with a mullet. Were those cross-country shorts from the like *Charlie's Angels* days or *quoi*? How could he run so well when he seemed to have literally no muscles? Every day he ran home like this, shirtless with his backpack on, then hit the remote from down by the Fungs' and scooted into his garage without breaking stride.

You almost had to admire the poor goof.

They'd grown up together, been little beaners in that mutual sandbox down by the creek. Hadn't they bathed together when wee or some such crud? She hoped that never got out. Because in terms of friends, Kyle was basically down to Feddy Slavko, who walked leaning way backward and was always retrieving things from between his teeth, announcing the name of the retrieved thing in Greek, then re-eating it. Kyle's mom and dad didn't let him do squat. He had to call home if the movie in World Culture might show bare boobs. Each of the items in his lunch box was clearly labeled.

Pas de bourrée.

And curtsy.

Pour quantity of Cheez Doodles into compartmentalized old-school Tupperware dealie.

Thanks, Mom, thanks, Dad. Your kitchen *rocks*.

Shake Tupperware dealie back and forth like panning for gold, then offer to some imaginary poor gathered round.

Please enjoy. Is there anything else I can do for you folks?

You have already done enough, Alison, by even deigning to speak to us.

That is so not true! Don't you understand, all people deserve respect? Each of us is a rainbow.

Uh, really? Look at this big open sore on my poor shriveled flank.

Allow me to fetch you some Vaseline.

That would be much appreciated. This thing kills.

But as far as that rainbow idea? She believed that. People were amazing. Mom was awesome, Dad was awesome, her teachers worked so hard and had kids of their own, and some were even getting divorced, such as Mrs. Dees, but still always took time for their students. What she found especially inspiring about Mrs. Dees was that, even though Mr. Dees was cheating on Mrs. Dees with the lady who ran the bowling alley, Mrs. Dees was still teaching the best course ever in Ethics, posing such questions as: Can goodness win? Or do good people always get shafted, evil being more reckless? That last bit seemed to be Mrs. Dees taking a shot at the bowling-alley gal. But seriously! Is life fun or scary? Are people good or bad? On the one hand, that clip of those gauntish pale bodies being steamrolled while fat German ladies looked on chomping gum. On the other hand, sometimes rural folks, even if their particular farms were on hills, stayed up late filling sandbags.

In their straw poll she had voted for people being good and life being fun, with Mrs. Dees giving her a pitying glance as she stated her views: To do good, you just have to decide to do good. You have to be brave. You have to stand up for what's right. At that last, Mrs. Dees had made this kind of groan. Which was fine. Mrs. Dees had a lot of pain in her life, yet, interestingly? Still obviously found something fun about life and good about people, because otherwise why sometimes stay up so late grading you come in next day all exhausted, blouse on backward, having messed it up in the early-morning dark, you dear discombobulated thing?

Here came a knock on the door. Back door. In-ter-est-ing. Who could it be? Father Dmitri from across the way? UPS? FedEx? With *un petit* check *pour Papa*?

Jeté, jeté, rond de jambe.

Pas de bourrée.

Open door, and—

Here was a man she did not know. Quite huge fellow, in one of those meter-reader vests.

Something told her to step back in, slam the door. But that seemed rude.

Instead she froze, smiled, did {eyebrow raise} to indicate: May I help you?

Kyle Boot dashed through the garage, into the living area, where the big clocklike wooden indicator was set at All Out. Other choices included: Mom & Dad Out; Mom Out; Dad Out; Kyle Out; Mom & Kyle Out; Dad & Kyle Out; and All In.

Why did they even need All In? Wouldn't they know it when they were All In? Would he like to ask Dad that? Who, in his excellent totally silent downstairs woodshop, had designed and built the Family Status Indicator?

Ha.

Ha ha.

On the kitchen island was a Work Notice.

Scout: New geode on deck. Place in yard per included drawing. No goofing. Rake areas first, put down plastic as I have shown you. Then lay in white rock. THIS GEODE EXPENSIVE. Pls take seriously. No reason this should not be done by time I get home. This = five (5) Work Points.

Gar, Dad, do you honestly feel it fair that I should have to slave in the yard until dark after a rigorous cross-country practice that included sixteen 440s, eight 880s, a mile-for-time, a kajillion Drake sprints, and a five-mile Indian relay?

Shoes off, mister.

Yoinks, too late. He was already at the TV. And had left an incriminating trail of microclods. Way verboten. Could the microclods be hand-plucked? Although, problem: if he went back to hand-pluck the microclods, he'd leave an incriminating new trail of microclods.

He took off his shoes and stood mentally rehearsing a little show he liked to call WHAT IF . . . RIGHT NOW?

WHAT IF they came home RIGHT NOW?

It's a funny story, Dad! I came in thoughtlessly! Then realized what I'd done! I guess, when I think about it, what I'm happy about? Is how quickly I self-corrected! The reason I came in so thoughtlessly was, I wanted to get right to work, Dad, per your note!

He raced in his socks to the garage, threw his shoes into the garage, ran for the vacuum, vacuumed up the microclods, then realized, holy golly, he had thrown his shoes into the garage rather than placing them on the Shoe Sheet as required, toes facing away from the door for ease of donnage later.

He stepped into the garage, placed his shoes on the Shoe Sheet, stepped back inside.

Scout, Dad said in his head, has anyone ever told you that even the most neatly maintained garage is going to have some oil on its floor, which is now on your socks, being tracked all over the tan Berber?

Oh gar, his ass was grass.

But no—*celebrate good times, come on*—no oil stain on rug.

He tore off his socks. It was absolutely verboten for him to be in the main living area barefoot. Mom and Dad coming home to find him Tarzaning around like some sort of white trasher would not be the least fucking bit—

Swearing in your head? Dad said in his head. Step up, Scout, be a man. If you want to swear, swear aloud.

I don't want to swear aloud.

Then don't swear in your head.

Mom and Dad would be heartsick if they could hear the swearing he sometimes did in his head, such as crap-cunt shit-turd dick-in-the-ear butt-creamery. Why couldn't he stop doing that? They thought so highly of him, sending weekly braggy emails to both sets of grandparents, such as: Kyle's been super-busy keeping up his grades while running varsity cross-country though still a sophomore, while setting aside a little time each day to manufacture such humdingers as cunt-swoggle rear-fuck—

What was wrong with him? Why couldn't he be grateful for all that Mom and Dad did for him, instead of

Cornhole the ear-cunt.

Flake-fuck the pale vestige with a proddering dick-knee.

You could always clear the mind with a hard pinch on your own minimal love handle.

Ouch.

Hey, today was Tuesday, a Major Treat day. The five (5) new Work Points for placing the geode, plus his existing two (2) Work Points, totaled seven (7) Work Points, which, added to his eight (8) accrued Usual Chore Points, made fifteen (15) Total Treat Points, which could garner him a Major Treat (for example, two handfuls of yogurt-covered raisins) plus twenty free-choice TV minutes, although the particular show would have to be negotiated with Dad at time of cash-in.

One thing you will not be watching, Scout, is *America's Most Outspoken Dirt Bikers*.

Whatever.

Whatever, Dad.

Really, Scout? "Whatever"? Will it be "whatever" when I take away all your Treat Points and force you to quit cross-country, as I have several times threatened to do if a little more cheerful obedience wasn't forthcoming?

No, no, no. I don't want to quit, Dad. Please. I'm good at it. You'll see, first meet. Even Matt Drey said—

Who is Matt Drey? Some ape on the football team?

Yes.

Is his word law?

No.

What did he say?

Little shit can run.

Nice talk, Scout. Ape talk. Anyway, you may not make it to the first meet. Your ego seems to be overflowing its banks. And why? Because you can jog? Anyone can jog. Beasts of the field can jog.

I'm not quitting! Anal-cock shit-bird rectum-fritz! Please, I'm begging you, it's the only thing I'm decent at! Mom, if he makes me quit I swear to God I'll—

Drama doesn't suit you, Beloved Only.

If you want the privilege of competing in a team sport, Scout, show us that you can live within our perfectly reasonable system of directives designed to benefit you.

Hello.

A van had just pulled up in the St. Mikhail's parking lot.

Kyle walked in a controlled, gentlemanly manner to the kitchen counter. On the counter was Kyle's Traffic Log, which served the dual purpose of (1) buttressing Dad's argument that Father Dmitri should build a soundproof retaining wall and (2) constituting a data set for a possible Science Fair project for him, Kyle, entitled, by Dad, "Correlation of Church Parking Lot Volume vs. Day of Week, with Ancillary Investigation of Sunday Volume Throughout Year."

Smiling agreeably as if he enjoyed filling out the Log, Kyle very legibly filled out the Log:

Vehicle: VAN.
Color: GRAY.
Make: CHEVY.
Year: UNKNOWN.

A guy got out of the van. One of the usual Rooskies. "Rooskie" was an allowed slang. Also "dang it." Also "holy golly." Also "crapper." The Rooskie was wearing a jean jacket over a hoodie, which, in Kyle's experience, was not unusual church-wear for the Rooskies, who sometimes came directly over from Jiffy Lube still wearing coveralls.

Under "Vehicle Driver" he wrote, PROBABLE PARISHIONER.

That sucked. Stank, rather. The guy being a stranger, he, Kyle, now had to stay inside until the stranger left the neighborhood. Which totally futzed up his geode placing. He'd be out there until midnight. What a detriment!

The guy put on a Day Glo-vest. Ah, dude was a meter reader.

The meter reader looked left, then right, leaped across the creek, entered the Pope backyard, passed between the soccer-ball rebounder and the in-ground pool, then knocked on the Pope door.

Good leap there, Boris.

The door swung open.

Alison.

Kyle's heart was singing. He'd always thought that was just a phrase. Alison was like a national treasure. In the dictionary under "beauty" there should be a picture of her in that jean skort. Although lately she didn't seem to like him all that much.

Now she stepped across her deck so the meter reader could show her something. Something electrical wrong on the roof? The guy seemed eager to show her. Actually, he had her by the wrist. And was like tugging.

That was weird. Wasn't it? Something had never been weird around here before. So probably it was fine. Probably the guy was just a really new meter reader?

Somehow Kyle felt like stepping out onto the deck. He stepped out. The guy froze. Alison's eyes were scared-horse eyes. The guy cleared his throat, turned slightly to let Kyle see something.

A knife.

The meter reader had a knife.

Here's what you're doing, the guy said. Standing right there until we leave. Move a muscle, I knife her in the heart. Swear to God. Got it?

Kyle's mouth was so spitless all he could do was make his mouth do the shape it normally did when saying Yes.

Now they were crossing the yard. Alison threw herself to the ground. The guy hauled her up. She threw herself down. He hauled her up. It was odd seeing Alison tossed like a rag doll in the sanctuary of the perfect yard her dad had made for her. She threw herself down.

The guy hissed something and she rose, suddenly docile.

In his chest Kyle felt the many directives, Major and Minor, he was right now violating. He was on the deck shoeless, on the deck shirtless, was outside when a stranger was near, had engaged with that stranger.

Last week Sean Ball had brought a wig to school to more effectively mimic the way Bev Mirren chewed her hair when nervous. Kyle had briefly considered intervening. At Evening Meeting, Mom had said that she considered Kyle's decision not to intervene judicious. Dad had said, That was none of your business. You could have been badly hurt. Mom had said, Think of all the resources we've invested in you, Beloved Only. Dad had said, I know we sometimes strike you as strict but you are literally all we have.

They were at the soccer-ball rebounder now, Alison's arm up behind her back. She was making a low repetitive sound of denial, like she was trying to invent a noise that would adequately communicate her feelings about what she'd just this instant realized was going to happen to her.

He was just a kid. There was nothing he could do. In his chest he felt the lush release of pressure that always resulted when he submitted to a directive. There at his feet was the geode. He should just look at that until they left. It was a great one. Maybe the greatest one ever. The crystals at the cutaway glistened in the sun. It would look nice in the yard. Once he placed it. He'd place it once they were gone. Dad would be impressed that even after what had occurred he'd remembered to place the geode.

That's the ticket, Scout.

We are well pleased, Beloved Only.

Super job, Scout.

Holy crap. It was happening. She was marching along all meek like the trouper he'd known she'd be. He'd had her in mind since the baptism of what's-his-name. Sergei's kid. At the Russian church. She'd been standing in her yard, her dad or some such taking her picture.

He'd been like, Hello, Betty.

Kenny had been like, Little young, bro.

He'd been like, For you, grandpa.

When you studied history, the history of cultures, you saw your own individual time as hidebound. There were various theories of acquiescence. In Bible days a king might ride through a field and go: That one. And she would be brought unto him. And they would duly be betrothed and if she gave birth unto a son, super, bring out the streamers, she was a keeper. Was she, that first night, digging it? Probably not. Was she shaking like a leaf? Didn't matter. What mat-

tered was offspring and the furtherance of the lineage. Plus
the exaltation of the king, which resulted in righteous kingly
power.

Here was the creek.

He marched her through.

The following bullet points remained in the decision matrix: take to side van door, shove in, follow in, tape wrists/
mouth, hook to chain, make speech. He had the speech
down cold. Had practiced it both in his head and on the re-
corder: *Calm your heart, darling, I know you're scared because you don't know me yet and didn't expect this today
but give me a chance and you will see we will fly high. See I
am putting the knife right over here and I don't expect I'll
have to use it, right?*

If she wouldn't get in the van, punch hard in gut. Then
pick up, carry to side van door, throw in, tape wrists/mouth,
hook to chain, make speech, etc., etc.

Stop, pause, he said.

Gal stopped.

Fucksake. Side door of the van was locked. How undisci-
plined was that. Ensuring that the door was unlocked was
clearly indicated on the pre-mission matrix. Melvin appeared in his mind. On Melvin's face was the look of hot
disappointment that had always preceded an ass whooping,
which had always preceded the other thing. Put up your
hands, Melvin said, defend yourself.

True, true. Little error there. Should have double-checked
the pre-mission matrix.

No biggie.

Joy not fear.

Melvin was dead fifteen years. Mom dead twelve.

Little bitch was turned around now, looking back at the house. That willfulness wouldn't stand. That was going to get nipped in the bud. He'd have to remember to hurt her early, establish a baseline.

Turn the fuck around, he said.

She turned around.

He unlocked the door, swung it open. Moment of truth. If she got in, let him use the tape, they were home free. He'd picked out a place in Sackett, big-ass cornfield, dirt road leading in. If fuckwise it went good they'd pick up the freeway from there. Basically steal the van. It was Kenny's van. He'd borrowed it for the day. Screw Kenny. Kenny had once called him stupid. Too bad, Kenny, that remark just cost you one van. If fuckwise it went bad, she didn't properly arouse him, he'd abort the activity, truncate the subject, heave the thing out, clean van as necessary, go buy corn, return van to Kenny, say, Hey, bro, here's a shitload of corn, thanks for the van, I never could've bought a suitable quantity of corn in my car. Then lay low, watch the papers like he'd done with the nonarousing redhead out in—

Gal gave him an imploring look, like, Please don't.

Was this a good time? To give her one in the gut, knock the wind out of her sails?

It was.

He did.

The geode was beautiful. What a beautiful geode. What made it beautiful? What were the principal characteristics of a beautiful geode? Come on, think. Come on, concentrate.

She'll recover in time, Beloved Only.

None of our affair, Scout.

We're amazed by your good judgment, Beloved Only.

Dimly he noted that Alison had been punched. Eyes on the geode, he heard the little *oof*.

His heart dropped at the thought of what he was letting happen. They'd used goldfish snacks as coins. They'd made bridges out of rocks. Down by the creek. Back in the day. Oh God. He should've never stepped outside. Once they were gone he'd just go back inside, pretend he'd never stepped out, make the model-railroad town, still be making it when Mom and Dad got home. When eventually someone told him about it? He'd make a certain face. Already on his face he could feel the face he would make, like, What? Alison? Raped? Killed? Oh God. Raped and killed while I innocently made my railroad town, sitting cross-legged and unaware on the floor like a tiny little—

No. No, no, no. They'd be gone soon. Then he could go inside. Call 911. Although then everyone would know he'd done nothing. All his future life would be bad. Forever he'd be the guy who'd done nothing. Besides, calling wouldn't do any good. They'd be long gone. The parkway was just across Featherstone, with like a million arteries and cloverleafs or whatever spouting out of it. So that was that. In he'd go. As soon as they left. Leave, leave, leave, he thought, so I can go inside, forget this ever—

Then he was running. Across the lawn. Oh God! What was he doing, what was he doing? Jesus, shit, the directives he was violating! Running in the yard (bad for the sod); transporting a geode without its protective wrapping; hopping the fence, which stressed the fence, which had cost a pretty penny; leaving the yard; leaving the yard barefoot; entering the Secondary Area without permission; entering the creek barefoot (broken glass, dangerous microorganisms), and, not only that, oh God, suddenly he saw what this giddy part of himself intended, which was to violate a directive so Major and absolute that it wasn't even a directive, since you didn't need a directive to know how totally verboten it was to—

He burst out of the creek, the guy still not turning, and let the geode fly into his head, which seemed to emit a weird edge-seep of blood even before the skull visibly indented and the guy sat right on his ass.

Yes! Score! It was fun! Fun dominating a grown-up! Fun using the most dazzling gazelle-like leg speed ever seen in the history of mankind to dash soundlessly across space and master this huge galoot, who otherwise, right now, would be—

What if he hadn't?

God, what if he hadn't?

He imagined the guy bending Alison in two like a pale garment bag while pulling her hair and thrusting bluntly, as he, Kyle, sat cowed and obedient, tiny railroad viaduct grasped in his pathetic babyish—

Jesus! He skipped over and hurled the geode through the windshield of the van, which imploded, producing an inward rain of glass shards that made the sound of thousands of tiny bamboo wind chimes.

He scrambled up the hood of the van, retrieved the geode.

Really? Really? You were going to ruin her life, ruin my life, you cunt-probe dick-munch ass-gashing Animal? Who's bossing who now? Gash-ass, jizz-lips, turd-munch—

He'd never felt so strong/angry/wild. Who's the man? Who's your daddy? What else must he do? To ensure that Animal did no further harm? You still moving, freak? Got a plan, stroke-dick? Want a skull gash on top of your existing skull gash, big man? You think I won't? You think I—

Easy, Scout, you're out of control.

Slow your motor down, Beloved Only.

Quiet. I'm the boss of me.

FUCK!

What the hell? What was he doing on the ground? Had he tripped? Did someone wonk him? Did a branch fall? God damn. He touched his head. His hand came away bloody.

The beanpole kid was bending. To pick something up. A rock. Why was that kid off the porch? Where was the knife?

Where was the gal?

Crab-crawling toward the creek.

Flying across her yard.

Going into her house.

Fuck it, everything was fucked. Better hit the road. With what, his good looks? He had like eight bucks total.

Ah Christ! The kid had smashed the windshield! With the rock! Kenny was not going to like that one bit.

He tried to stand but couldn't. The blood was just pouring out. He was not going to jail again. No way. He'd slit his wrists. Where was the knife? He'd stab himself in the chest. That had nobility. Then the people would know his name. Which of them had the balls to samurai themselves with a knife in the chest?

None.

Nobody.

Go ahead, pussy. Do it.

No. The king does not take his own life. The superior man silently accepts the mindless rebuke of the rabble. Waits to rise and fight anew. Plus he had no idea where the knife was. Well, he didn't need it. He'd crawl into the woods, kill something with his bare hands. Or make a trap from some grass. Ugh. Was he going to barf? There, he had. Right on his lap.

Figures you'd blow the simplest thing, Melvin said.

Melvin, God, can't you see my head is bleeding so bad?

A kid did it to you. You're a joke. You got fucked by a kid.

Oh, sirens, perfect.

Well, it was a sad day for the cops. He'd fight them hand to hand. He'd sit until the last moment, watching them draw near, doing a silent death mantra that would centralize all his life power in his fists.

He sat thinking about his fists. They were huge granite boulders. They were a pit bull each. He tried to get up. Somehow his legs weren't working. He hoped the cops would get here soon. His head really hurt. When he touched up there, things moved. It was like he was wearing a gore cap. He was going to need a bunch of stitches. He hoped it wouldn't hurt too much. Probably it would, though.

Where was that beanpole kid?

Oh, here he was.

Looming over him, blocking out the sun, rock held high, yelling something, but he couldn't tell what, because of the ringing in his ears.

Then he saw that the kid was going to bring the rock down. He closed his eyes and waited and was not at peace at all but instead felt the beginnings of a terrible dread welling up inside him, and if that dread kept growing at the current rate, he realized in a flash of insight, there was a name for the place he would be then, and it was Hell.

Alison stood at the kitchen window. She'd peed herself. Which was fine. People did that. When super-scared. She'd noticed it while making the call. Her hands had been shaking so bad. They still were. One leg was doing that Thumper thing. God, the stuff he'd said to her. He'd punched her. He'd pinched her. There was a big blue mark on her arm.

How could Kyle still be out there? But there he was, in those comical shorts, so confident he was goofing around, hands clenched over his head like a boxer from some cute alt universe where a kid that skinny could actually win a fight against a guy with a knife.

Wait.

His hands weren't clenched. He was holding the rock, shouting something down at the guy, who was on his knees, like the blindfolded prisoner in that video they'd seen in History, about to get sword-killed by a formal dude in a helmet.

Kyle, don't, she whispered.

For months afterward she had nightmares in which Kyle brought the rock down. She was on the deck trying to scream his name but nothing was coming out. Down came the rock. Then the guy had no head. The blow just literally dissolved his head. Then his body tumped over and Kyle turned to her with this heartbroken look of, My life is over. I killed a guy.

Why was it, she sometimes wondered, that in dreams we can't do the simplest things? Like a crying puppy is standing on some broken glass and you want to pick it up and brush the shards off its pads but you can't because you're balancing a ball on your head. Or you're driving and there's this old guy on crutches, and you go, to Mr. Feder, your Driver's Ed teacher, Should I swerve? And he's like, Uh, probably. But then you hear this big clunk and Feder makes a negative mark in his book.

Sometimes she'd wake up crying from the dream about Kyle. The last time, Mom and Dad were already there, going, That's not how it was. Remember, Allie? How did it happen? Say it. Say it out loud. Allie, can you tell Mommy and Daddy how it really happened?

I ran outside, she said. I shouted.

That's right, Dad said. You shouted. Shouted like a champ.

And what did Kyle do? Mom said.

Put down the rock, she said.

A bad thing happened to you kids, Dad said. But it could have been worse.

So much worse, Mom said.

But because of you kids, Dad said, it wasn't.

You did so good, Mom said.

Did beautiful, Dad said.

STICKS

Every year Thanksgiving night we flocked out behind Dad
as he dragged the Santa suit to the road and draped it over a
kind of crucifix he'd built out of metal pole in the yard. Super
Bowl week the pole was dressed in a jersey and Rod's helmet
and Rod had to clear it with Dad if he wanted to take the
helmet off. On Fourth of July the pole was Uncle Sam, on
Veterans Day a soldier, on Halloween a ghost. The pole was
Dad's one concession to glee. We were allowed a single Cray-
ola from the box at a time. One Christmas Eve he shrieked
at Kimmie for wasting an apple slice. He hovered over us as
we poured ketchup, saying, Good enough good enough
good enough. Birthday parties consisted of cupcakes, no ice

cream. The first time I brought a date over she said, What's with your dad and that pole? and I sat there blinking.

We left home, married, had children of our own, found the seeds of meanness blooming also within us. Dad began dressing the pole with more complexity and less discernible logic. He draped some kind of fur over it on Groundhog Day and lugged out a floodlight to ensure a shadow. When an earthquake struck Chile he laid the pole on its side and spray-painted a rift in the earth. Mom died and he dressed the pole as Death and hung from the crossbar photos of Mom as a baby. We'd stop by and find odd talismans from his youth arranged around the base: army medals, theater tickets, old sweatshirts, tubes of Mom's makeup. One autumn he painted the pole bright yellow. He covered it with cotton swabs that winter for warmth and provided offspring by hammering in six crossed sticks around the yard. He ran lengths of string between the pole and the sticks, and taped to the string letters of apology, admissions of error, pleas for understanding, all written in a frantic hand on index cards. He painted a sign saying LOVE and hung it from the pole and another that said FORGIVE? and then he died in the hall with the radio on and we sold the house to a young couple who yanked out the pole and left it by the road on garbage day.

PUPPY

Twice already Marie had pointed out the brilliance of the autumnal sun on the perfect field of corn, because the brilliance of the autumnal sun on the perfect field of corn put her in mind of a haunted house—not a haunted house she had ever actually seen but the mythical one that sometimes appeared in her mind (with adjacent graveyard and cat on a fence) whenever she saw the brilliance of the autumnal sun on the perfect etc., etc.—and she wanted to make sure that, if the kids had a corresponding mythical haunted house that appeared in their minds whenever they saw the brilliance of the etc., etc., it would come up now, so that they could all experience it together, like friends, like college friends on a road trip, sans pot, ha ha ha!

But no. When she, a third time, said, "Wow, guys, check that out," Abbie said, "Okay, Mom, we get it, it's corn," and Josh said, "Not now, Mom, I'm Leavening my Loaves," which was fine with her; she had no problem with that, Noble Baker being preferable to Bra Stuffer, the game he'd asked for.

Well, who could say? Maybe they didn't even have any mythical vignettes in their heads. Or maybe the mythical vignettes they had in their heads were totally different from the ones she had in her head. Which was the beauty of it, because, after all, they were their own little people! You were just a caretaker. They didn't have to feel what *you* felt; they just had to be supported in feeling what *they* felt.

Still, wow, that cornfield was such a classic.

"Whenever I see a field like that, guys?" she said. "I somehow think of a haunted house!"

"Slicing Knife! Slicing Knife!" Josh shouted. "You nimrod machine! I chose that!"

Speaking of Halloween, she remembered last year, when their cornstalk column had tipped their shopping cart over. Gosh, how they'd laughed at that! Oh, family laughter was golden; she'd had none of that in her childhood, Dad being so dour and Mom so ashamed. If Mom and Dad's cart had tipped, Dad would have given the cart a despairing kick and Mom would have stridden purposefully away to reapply her lipstick, distancing herself from Dad, while she, Marie, would have nervously taken that horrid plastic army man she'd named Brady into her mouth.

Well, in this family laughter was encouraged! Last night, when Josh had goosed her with his Game Boy, she'd shot a spray of toothpaste across the mirror and they'd all cracked up, rolling around on the floor with Goochie, and Josh had said, such nostalgia in his voice, "Mom, remember when Goochie was a puppy?" Which was when Abbie had burst into tears, because, being only five, she had no memory of Goochie as a puppy.

Hence this Family Mission. And as far as Robert? Oh, God bless Robert! There was a man. He would have no problem whatsoever with this Family Mission. She loved the way he had of saying "Ho HO!" whenever she brought home something new and unexpected.

"Ho HO!" Robert had said, coming home to find the iguana. "Ho HO!" he had said, coming home to find the ferret trying to get into the iguana cage. "We appear to be the happy operators of a menagerie!"

She loved him for his playfulness—you could bring home a hippo you'd put on a credit card (both the ferret and the iguana had gone on credit cards) and he'd just say, "Ho HO!" and ask what the creature ate and what hours it slept and what the heck they were going to name the little bugger.

In the backseat, Josh made the *git-git-git* sound he always made when his Baker was in Baking Mode, trying to get his Loaves into the oven while fighting off various Hungry Denizens, such as a Fox with a distended stomach; such as a fey Robin that would improbably carry the Loaf away, speared on its beak, whenever it had succeeded in dropping a Clonking Rock on your Baker—all of which Marie had learned over the summer by studying the Noble Baker manual while Josh was asleep.

And it had helped, it really had. Josh was less withdrawn lately, and when she came up behind him now while he was playing and said, like, "Wow, honey, I didn't know you could do Pumpernickel," or "Sweetie, try Serrated Blade, it cuts quicker. Try it while doing Latch the Window," he would reach back with his noncontrolling hand and swat at her affectionately, and yesterday they'd shared a good laugh when he'd accidentally knocked off her glasses.

So her mother could go right ahead and claim that she was spoiling the kids. These were not spoiled kids. These were *well-loved* kids. At least she'd never left one of them standing in a blizzard for two hours after a junior-high dance. At least she'd never drunkenly snapped at one of them, "I hardly consider you college material." At least she'd never locked one of them in a closet (a closet!) while entertaining a literal ditchdigger in the parlor.

Oh, God, what a beautiful world! The autumn colors, that glinting river, that lead-colored cloud pointing down like a rounded arrow at that half-remodeled McDonald's standing above I-90 like a castle.

This time would be different, she was sure of it. The kids would care for this pet themselves, since a puppy wasn't scaly and didn't bite. ("Ho HO!" Robert had said the first time the iguana bit him. "I see you have an opinion on the matter!")

Thank you, Lord, she thought, as the Lexus flew through the cornfield. You have given me so much: struggles and the strength to overcome them; grace, and new chances every day to spread that grace around. And in her mind she sang out, as she sometimes did when feeling that the world was good and she had at last found her place in it, "Ho HO, ho HO!"

Callie pulled back the blind.

Yes. Awesome. It was still solved so *perfect.*

There was plenty for him to do back there. A yard could be a whole world. Like her yard when she was a kid had been a whole world. From the three holes in their wood fence she'd been able to see Exxon (Hole One) and Accident Corner (Hole Two), and Hole Three was actually two holes that if you lined them up right your eyes would do this weird crossing thing and you could play Oh My God I Am So High by staggering away with your eyes crossed, going, "Peace, man, peace."

When Bo got older, it would be different. Then he'd need his freedom. But now he just needed not to get killed. Once they'd found him way over on Testament. And that was across I-90. How had he crossed I-90? She knew how. Darted. That's how he crossed streets. Once a total stranger had called them from Hightown Plaza. Even Dr. Brile had said it: "Callie, this boy is going to end up dead if you don't get this under control. Is he taking the medications?"

Well, he was and he wasn't. The meds made him grind his teeth and his fist would suddenly pound down. He'd broken plates that way, and once a glass tabletop and got four stitches in his wrist.

Today he didn't need the meds because he was safe in the yard, because she'd fixed it so *perfect*.

He was out there practicing pitching by filling his Yankees helmet with pebbles and winging them at the tree.

He looked up and saw her and did the thing where he blew a kiss.

Sweet little man.

Now all she had to worry about was the pup. She hoped the lady who'd called would actually show up. It was a nice pup. White, with brown around one eye. Cute. If the lady showed up, she'd definitely want it. And if she took it, Jimmy was off the hook. He'd hated doing it that time with the kittens. But if no one took the pup he'd do it. He'd have to. Because his feeling was, when you said you were going to do a thing and didn't do it, that was how kids got into drugs. Plus he'd been raised on a farm, or near a farm anyways, and anybody raised on a farm knew you had to do what you had to do in terms of sick animals or extra animals—the pup being not sick, just extra.

That time with the kittens, Brianna and Jessi had called him a murderer, getting Bo all worked up, and Jimmy had yelled, "Look, you kids, I was raised on a farm and you got to do what you got to do!" Then he'd cried in bed, saying how the kittens had mewed in the bag all the way to the pond, and how he wished he'd never been raised on a farm, and she'd almost said, "You mean near a farm" (his dad had run a car wash outside Cortland), but sometimes when she got too smart-assed he would do this hard pinching thing on her arm while waltzing her around the bedroom, as if the place where he was pinching was like her handle, going, "I'm not sure I totally heard what you just said."

So, that time after the kittens, she'd only said, "Oh, honey, you did what you had to do."

And he'd said, "I guess I did, but it's sure not easy raising kids the right way."

And then, because she hadn't made his life harder by being a smart-ass, they had lain there making plans, like why not sell this place and move to Arizona and buy a car wash, why not buy the kids Hooked on Phonics, why not plant tomatoes, and then they'd got to wrestling around and (she had no idea why she remembered this) he'd done this thing of, while holding her close, bursting this sudden laugh/ despair-snort into her hair, like a sneeze, or like he was about to start crying.

Which had made her feel special, him trusting her with that.

So what she'd love, for tonight? Was getting the pup sold, putting the kids to bed early, and then, Jimmy seeing her as all organized in terms of the pup, they could mess around and afterward lie there making plans, and he could do that laugh/snort thing in her hair again.

Why that laugh/snort meant so much to her she had no

freaking idea. It was just one of the weird things about the Wonder That Was Her, ha ha ha.

Outside, Bo hopped to his feet, suddenly curious, because (here we go) the lady who'd called had just pulled up?

Yep, and in a nice car, too, which meant too bad she'd put "Cheap" in the ad.

Abbie squealed, "I love it, Mommy, I want it!" as the puppy looked up dimly from its shoebox and the lady of the house went trudging away and one-two-three-four plucked up four *dog turds* from the rug.

Well, wow, what a super field trip for the kids, Marie thought, ha ha (the filth, the mildew smell, the dry aquarium holding the single encyclopedia volume, the pasta pot on the bookshelf with an inflatable candy cane inexplicably sticking out of it), and although some might have been disgusted (by the spare tire on the *dining-room table,* by the way the glum mother dog, the presumed in-house pooper, was now dragging her rear over the pile of clothing in the corner, in a sitting position, splay-legged, moronic look of pleasure on her face), Marie realized (resisting the urge to rush to the sink and wash her hands, in part because the sink had a *basketball* in it) that what this really was, was deeply sad.

Please do not touch anything, please do not touch, she said to Josh and Abbie, but just in her head, wanting to give the children a chance to observe her being democratic and accepting, and afterward they could all wash up at the half-remodeled McDonald's, as long as they just please please kept their hands out of their mouths, and God forbid they should rub their eyes.

The phone rang, and the lady of the house plodded into the kitchen, placing the daintily held, paper-towel-wrapped turds *on the counter.*

"Mommy, I want it," Abbie said.

"I will definitely walk him like twice a day," Josh said.

"Don't say 'like,'" Marie said.

"I will definitely walk him twice a day," Josh said.

Okay, then, all right, they would adopt a white-trash dog. Ha ha. They could name it Zeke, buy it a little corncob pipe and a straw hat. She imagined the puppy, having crapped on the rug, looking up at her, going, *Cain't hep it.* But no. Had she come from a perfect place? Everything was transmutable. She imagined the puppy grown up, entertaining some friends, speaking to them in a British accent: *My family of origin was, um, rather not, shall we say, of the most respectable . . .*

Ha ha, wow, the mind was amazing, always cranking out these—

Marie stepped to the window and, anthropologically pulling the blind aside, was shocked, so shocked that she dropped the blind and shook her head, as if trying to wake herself, shocked to see a young boy, just a few years younger than Josh, harnessed and chained to a tree, via some sort of doohickey by which—she pulled the blind back again, sure she could not have seen what she thought she had—

When the boy ran, the chain spooled out. He was running now, looking back at her, showing off. When he reached the end of the chain, it jerked and he dropped as if shot.

He rose to a sitting position, railed against the chain, whipped it back and forth, crawled to a bowl of water, and, lifting it to his lips, took a drink: a drink *from a dog's bowl*.

Josh joined her at the window.

She let him look.

He should know that the world was not all lessons and iguanas and Nintendo. It was also this muddy simple boy tethered like an animal.

She remembered coming out of the closet to find her mother's scattered lingerie and the ditchdigger's metal hanger full of orange flags. She remembered waiting outside the junior high in the bitter cold, the snow falling harder, as she counted over and over to two hundred, promising herself each time that when she reached two hundred she would begin the long walk back—

God, she would have killed for just one righteous adult to confront her mother, shake her, say, "You idiot, this is your child, your child you're—"

"So what were you guys thinking of naming him?" the woman said, coming out of the kitchen.

The cruelty and ignorance just radiated from her fat face, with its little smear of lipstick.

"I'm afraid we won't be taking him after all," Marie said coldly.

Such an uproar from Abbie! But Josh—she would have

to praise him later, maybe buy him the Italian Loaves Expansion Pak—hissed something to Abbie, and then they were moving out through the trashed kitchen (past some kind of *crankshaft* on a cookie sheet, past a partial red pepper afloat *in a can of green paint*) while the lady of the house scuttled after them, saying, wait, wait, they could have it free, please take it—she just really wanted them to have it.

No, Marie said, it would not be possible for them to take it at this time, her feeling being that one really shouldn't possess something if one wasn't up to properly caring for it.

"Oh," the woman said, slumping in the doorway, the scrambling pup on one shoulder.

Out in the Lexus, Abbie began to cry softly, saying, "Really, that was the perfect pup for me."

And it was a nice pup, but Marie was not going to contribute to a situation like this in even the smallest way.

Simply was not going to do it.

The boy came to the fence. If only she could say to him, with a single look, *Life will not necessarily always be like this. Your life could suddenly blossom into something wonderful. It can happen. It happened to me.*

But secret looks, looks that conveyed a world of meaning with their subtle blah blah blah—that was all bullshit. What was not bullshit was a call to Child Welfare, where she knew Linda Berling, a very no-nonsense lady who would snatch this poor kid away so fast it would make that fat mother's thick head spin.

Callie shouted, "Bo, back in a sec!" and, swiping the corn out of the way with her non-pup arm, walked until there was nothing but corn and sky.

It was so small it didn't move when she set it down, just sniffed and tumped over.

Well, what did it matter, drowned in a bag or starved in the corn? This way Jimmy wouldn't have to do it. He had enough to worry about. The boy she'd first met with hair to his waist was now this old man shrunk with worry. As far as the money, she had sixty hidden away. She'd give him twenty of that and go, "The people who bought the pup were super-nice."

Don't look back, don't look back, she said in her head as she raced away through the corn.

Then she was walking along Teallback Road like a sport-walker, like some lady who walked every night to get slim, except that she was nowhere near slim, she knew that, and also knew that when sportwalking you did not wear jeans and unlaced hiking boots. Ha ha. She wasn't stupid. She just made bad choices. She remembered Sister Lynette saying, "Callie, you are bright enough but you incline toward that which does not benefit you." *Yep, well, Sister, you got that right,* she said to the nun in her mind. But what the hell. What the heck. When things got easier moneywise, she'd get some decent tennis shoes and start walking and get slim. And start night school. Slimmer. Maybe medical technology. She was never going to be really slim. But Jimmy liked her the way she was. And she liked him the way he was. Which maybe that's what love was: liking someone how he was and doing things to help him get even better.

Like right now she was helping Jimmy by making his life easier by killing something so he—no. All she was doing was walking, walking away from—

What had she just said? That had been good. *Love was liking someone how he was and doing things to help him get even better.*

Like Bo wasn't perfect, but she loved him how he was and tried to help him get better. If they could keep him safe, maybe he'd mellow out as he got older. If he mellowed out, maybe he could someday have a family. Like there he was now in the yard, sitting quietly, looking at flowers. Tapping with his bat, happy enough. He looked up, waved the bat at her, gave her that smile. Yesterday he'd been stuck in the house, all miserable. He'd ended the day screaming in bed, so frustrated. Today he was looking at flowers. Who was it that thought up that idea, the idea that had made today better than yesterday? Who loved him enough to think that up? Who loved him more than anyone else in the world loved him?

Her.

She did.

ESCAPE FROM SPIDERHEAD

I

"Drip on?" Abnesti said over the P.A.

"What's in it?" I said.

"Hilarious," he said.

"Acknowledge," I said.

Abnesti used his remote. My MobiPak™ whirred. Soon the Interior Garden looked really nice. Everything seemed super-clear.

I said out loud, as I was supposed to, what I was feeling.

"Garden looks nice," I said. "Super-clear."

Abnesti said, "Jeff, how about we pep up those language centers?"

"Sure," I said.

"Drip on?" he said.

"Acknowledge," I said.

He added some Verbaluce™ to the drip, and soon I was feeling the same things but saying them better. The garden still looked nice. It was like the bushes were so tight-seeming and the sun made everything stand out? It was like any moment you expected some Victorians to wander in with their cups of tea. It was as if the garden had become a sort of embodiment of the domestic dreams forever intrinsic to human consciousness. It was as if I could suddenly discern, in this contemporary vignette, the ancient corollary through which Plato and some of his contemporaries might have strolled; to wit, I was sensing the eternal in the ephemeral.

I sat, pleasantly engaged in these thoughts, until the Verbaluce™ began to wane. At which point the garden just looked nice again. It was something about the bushes and whatnot? It made you just want to lay out there and catch rays and think your happy thoughts. If you get what I mean.

Then whatever else was in the drip wore off, and I didn't feel much about the garden one way or the other. My mouth was dry, though, and my gut had that post-Verbaluce™ feel to it.

"What's going to be cool about that one?" Abnesti said. "Is, say a guy has to stay up late guarding a perimeter. Or is at school waiting for his kid and gets bored. But there's some nature nearby? Or say a park ranger has to work a double shift?"

"That will be cool," I said.

"That's ED763," he said. "We're thinking of calling it NatuGlide. Or maybe ErthAdmire."

"Those are both good," I said.

"Thanks for your help, Jeff," he said.

Which was what he always said.

"Only a million years to go," I said.

Which was what I always said.

Then he said, "Exit the Interior Garden now, Jeff, head over to Small Workroom 2."

II

Into Small Workroom 2 they sent this pale tall girl.

"What do you think?" Abnesti said over the P.A.

"Me?" I said. "Or her?"

"Both," Abnesti said.

"Pretty good," I said.

"Fine, you know," she said. "Normal."

Abnesti asked us to rate each other more quantifiably, as per pretty, as per sexy.

It appeared we liked each other about average, i.e., no big attraction or revulsion either way.

Abnesti said, "Jeff, drip on?"

"Acknowledge," I said.

"Heather, drip on?" he said.

"Acknowledge," Heather said.

Then we looked at each other like, What happens next? What happened next was, Heather soon looked super-good. And I could tell she thought the same of me. It came on so sudden we were like laughing. How could we not have seen it, how cute the other one was? Luckily there was a couch in the Workroom. It felt like our drip had, in addition to whatever they were testing, some ED556 in it, which lowers your shame level to like nil. Because soon, there on the couch, off we went. It was super-hot between us. And not merely in a horndog way. Hot, yes, but also just right. Like if you'd dreamed of a certain girl all your life and all of a sudden there she was, in your same Workroom.

"Jeff," Abnesti said. "I'd like your permission to pep up your language centers."

"Go for it," I said, under her now.

"Drip on?" he said.

"Acknowledge," I said.

"Me, too?" Heather said.

"You got it," Abnesti said, with a laugh. "Drip on?"

"Acknowledge," she said, all breathless.

Soon, experiencing the benefits of the flowing Verbaluce™ in our drips, we were not only fucking really well but also talking pretty great. Like, instead of just saying the sex-type things we had been saying (such as "wow" and "oh God" and "hell yes" and so forth), we now began freestyling re our sensations and thoughts, in elevated diction, with eighty-percent increased vocab, our well-articulated thoughts being recorded for later analysis.

For me, the feeling was, approximately: astonishment at the dawning realization that this woman was being created in real time, directly from my own mind, per my deepest longings. Finally, after all these years (was my thought), I had found the precise arrangement of body/face/mind that personified all that was desirable. The taste of her mouth, the look of that halo of blondish hair spread out around her cherubic yet naughty-looking face (she was beneath me now, legs way up), even (not to be crude or dishonor the exalted feelings I was experiencing) the sensations her vagina was producing along the length of my thrusting penis were precisely those I had always hungered for, though I had never, before this instant, realized that I so ardently hungered for them.

That is to say: a desire would arise and, concurrently, the satisfaction of that desire would also arise. It was as if (a) I longed for a certain (heretofore untasted) taste until (b) said longing became nearly unbearable, at which time (c) I found a morsel of food with that exact taste already in my mouth, perfectly satisfying my longing.

Every utterance, every adjustment of posture bespoke the same thing: we had known each other forever, were soul mates, had met and loved in numerous preceding lifetimes, and would meet and love in many subsequent lifetimes, always with the same transcendently stupefying results.

Then there came a hard-to-describe but very real drifting

off into a number of sequential reveries that might best be described as a type of nonnarrative mind scenery, i.e., a series of vague mental images of places I had never been (a certain pine-packed valley in high white mountains; a chalet-type house in a cul-de-sac, the yard of which was overgrown with wide, stunted Seussian trees), each of which triggered a deep sentimental longing, longings that coalesced into, and were soon reduced to, one central longing, i.e., an intense longing for Heather and Heather alone.

This mind-scenery phenomenon was strongest during our third (!) bout of lovemaking. (Apparently, Abnesti had included some Vivistif™ in my drip.)

Afterward, our protestations of love poured forth simultaneously, linguistically complex and metaphorically rich: I daresay we had become poets. We were allowed to lie there, limbs intermingled, for nearly an hour. It was bliss. It was perfection. It was that impossible thing: happiness that does not wilt to reveal the thin shoots of some new desire rising from within it.

We cuddled with a fierceness/focus that rivaled the fierceness/focus with which we had fucked. There was nothing *less* about cuddling vis-à-vis fucking, is what I mean to say. We were all over each other in the super-friendly way of puppies, or spouses meeting for the first time after one of them has undergone a close brush with death. Everything seemed moist, permeable, *sayable*.

Then something in the drip began to wane. I think Abnesti had shut off the Verbaluce™? Also the shame reducer?

Basically, everything began to *dwindle*. Suddenly we felt shy. But still loving. We began the process of trying to talk après Verbaluce™: always awkward.

Yet I could see in her eyes that she was still feeling love for me.

And I was definitely still feeling love for her.

Well, why not? We had just fucked three times! Why do you think they call it "making love"? That is what we had just made three times: love.

Then Abnesti said, "Drip on?"

We had kind of forgotten he was even there behind his one-way mirror.

I said: "Do we have to? We are really liking this right now."

"We are just going to try to get you guys back to baseline," he said. "We've got more to do today."

"Shit," I said.

"Rats," she said.

"Drip on?" he said.

"Acknowledge," we said.

Soon, something began to change. I mean, she was fine. A handsome pale girl. But nothing special. And I could see that she felt the same re me, i.e.: What had all that fuss been about just now?

Why weren't we dressed? We real quick got dressed.

Kind of embarrassing.

Did I love her? Did she love me?

Ha.

No.

Then it was time for her to go. We shook hands.

Out she went.

Lunch came in. On a tray. Spaghetti with chicken chunks. Man, was I hungry.

I spent all lunchtime thinking. It was weird. I had the memory of fucking Heather, the memory of having felt the things I'd felt for her, the memory of having said the things I'd said to her. My throat was like raw from how much I'd said and how fast I'd felt compelled to say it. But in terms of feelings? I basically had nada left.

Just a hot face and some shame re having fucked three times in front of Abnesti.

III

After lunch in came another girl.

About equally so-so. Dark hair. Average build. Nothing special, just like, upon first entry, Heather had been nothing special.

"This is Rachel," Abnesti said on the P.A. "This is Jeff."

"Hi, Rachel," I said.

"Hi, Jeff," she said.

"Drip on?" Abnesti said.

We Acknowledged.

Something felt very familiar about the way I now began

feeling. Suddenly Rachel looked super-good. Abnesti requested permission to pep up our language centers via Verbaluce™. We Acknowledged. Soon we, too, were fucking like bunnies. Soon we, too, were talking like articulate maniacs re our love. Once again certain sensations were arising to meet my concurrently arising desperate hunger for just those sensations. Soon my memory of the perfect taste of Heather's mouth was being overwritten by the current taste of Rachel's mouth, so much more the taste I now desired. I was feeling unprecedented emotions, even though those unprecedented emotions were (I discerned somewhere in my consciousness) exactly the *same emotions* I had felt earlier, for that now unworthy-seeming vessel Heather. Rachel was, I mean to say, *it*. Her lithe waist, her voice, her hungry mouth/hands/loins—they were all *it*.

I just loved Rachel so much.

Then came the sequential geographic reveries (see above): same pine-packed valley, same chalet-looking house, accompanied by that same longing-for-place transmuting into a longing-for (this time) Rachel. While continuing to enact a level of sexual strenuousness that caused what I would describe as a gradually tightening, chest-located, sweetness rubber band to both connect us and compel us onward, we whispered feverishly (precisely, poetically) about how long we felt we had known each other, i.e., forever.

Again the total number of times we made love was three.

Then, like before, came the dwindling. Our talking became less excellent. Words were fewer, our sentences shorter.

Still, I loved her. Loved Rachel. Everything about her just seemed *perfect*: her cheek mole, her black hair, the little butt squirm she did now and then, as if to say: Mmm-mmm, was that ever good.

"Drip on?" Abnesti said. "We are going to try to get you both back to baseline."

"Acknowledge," she said.

"Well, hold on," I said.

"Jeff," Abnesti said, irritated, as if trying to remind me that I was not here by choice but because I had done my crime and was in the process of doing my time.

"Acknowledge," I said. And gave Rachel one last look of love, knowing (as she did not yet know) that this would be the last look of love I would be giving her.

Soon she was merely fine to me, and I merely fine to her. She looked, as had Heather, embarrassed, as in: What was up with that just now? Why did I just go so overboard with Mr. Average here?

Did I love her? Or her me?

No.

When it was time for her to go, we shook hands.

The place where my MobiPak™ was surgically joined to my lower back was sore from all our positional changes. Plus I was way tired. Plus I was feeling so sad. Why sad? Was I not a dude? Had I not just fucked two different girls, for a total of six times, in one day?

Still, honestly, I felt sadder than sad.

I guess I was sad that love was not real? Or not all that

real, anyway? I guess I was sad that love could feel so real and the next minute be gone, and all because of something Abnesti was doing.

IV

After Snack Abnesti called me into Control. Control being like the head of a spider. With its various legs being our Workrooms. Sometimes we were called upon to work along- side Abnesti in the head of the spider. Or, as we termed it: the Spiderhead.

"Sit," he said. "Look into Large Workroom 1."

In Large Workroom 1 were Heather and Rachel, side by side.

"Recognize them?" he said.

"Ha," I said.

"Now," Abnesti said. "I'm going to present you with a choice, Jeff. This is what we're playing at here. See this re- mote? Let's say you can hit *this* button and Rachel gets some Darkenfloxx™. Or you can hit *this* button and Heather gets the Darkenfloxx™. See? You choose."

"They've got Darkenfloxx™ in their MobiPaks™?" I said.

"You've all got Darkenfloxx™ in your MobiPaks™, dummy," Abnesti said affectionately. "Verlaine put it there Wednesday. In anticipation of this very study."

Well, that made me nervous.

Imagine the worst you have ever felt, times ten. That does not even come close to how bad you feel on Darkenfloxx™. The time it was administered to us in Orientation, briefly, for demo purposes, at one-third the dose now selected on Abnesti's remote? I have never felt so terrible. All of us were just moaning, heads down, like, How could we ever have felt life was worth living?

I do not even like to think about that time.

"What's your decision, Jeff?" Abnesti said. "Is Rachel getting the Darkenfloxx™? Or Heather?"

"I can't say," I said.

"You have to," he said.

"I can't," I said. "It would be like random."

"You feel your decision would be random," he said.

"Yes," I said.

And that was true. I really didn't care. It was like if I put *you* in the Spiderhead and gave you the choice: Which of these two strangers would you like to send into the shadow of the valley of death?

"Ten seconds," Abnesti said. "What we're testing for here is any residual fondness."

It wasn't that I liked them both. I honestly felt completely neutral toward both. It was as if I had never seen, much less fucked, either one. (They had really succeeded in taking me back to baseline, I guess I am saying.)

But, having once been Darkenfloxxed™, I just didn't want to do that to anyone. Even if I didn't like the person very much, even if I hated the person, I still wouldn't want to do it.

"Five seconds," Abnesti said.

"I can't decide," I said. "It's random."

"Truly random?" he said. "Okay. I'm giving the Darken-floxx™ to Heather."

I just sat there.

"No, actually," he said, "I'm giving it to Rachel."

Just sat there.

"Jeff," he said. "You have convinced me. It would, to you, be random. You truly have no preference. I can see that. And therefore I don't have to do it. See what we just did? With your help? For the first time? Via the ED289/290 suite? Which is what we've been testing today? You have to admit it: you were in love. Twice. Right?"

"Yes," I said.

"Very much in love," he said. "Twice."

"I said yes," I said.

"But you just now expressed no preference," he said. "Ergo, no trace of either of those great loves remains. You are totally cleansed. We brought you high, laid you low, and now here you sit, the same emotion-wise as before our testing even began. That is powerful, that is killer. We have unlocked a mysterious eternal secret. What a fantastic game changer. Say someone can't love? Now he or she can. We can make him. Say someone loves too much? Or loves someone deemed unsuitable by his or her caregiver? We can tone that shit right down. Say someone is blue, because of true love? We step in, or his or her caregiver does: blue no more. No longer, in terms of emotional controllability, are we ships adrift. No one is. We see a ship adrift, we climb aboard, install a rudder. Guide him/her toward love. Or away from it. You say, 'All you need is love'? Look, here comes ED289/290. Can we stop war? We can sure as heck slow it down! Suddenly the soldiers on both sides start fucking. Or, at low dosage, feeling superfond. Or say we have two rival dictators in a death grudge. Assuming ED289/290 develops nicely in pill form, allow me to slip each dictator a mickey. Soon their tongues are down each other's throats and doves of peace are pooping on their epaulets. Or, depending on the dosage, they may just be hugging. And who helped us do that? You did."

All this time, Rachel and Heather had just been sitting there in Large Workroom 1.

"That's it gals, thanks," Abnesti said on the P.A.

And they left, neither knowing how close they had come to getting Darkenfloxxed™ out their wing-wangs.

Verlaine took them out the back way, i.e., not through the Spiderhead but via the Back Alley. Which is not really an alley, just a carpeted hallway leading back to our Domain Cluster.

"Think, Jeff," Abnesti said. "Think if you'd had the benefit of ED289/290 on your fateful night."

Tell the truth, I was getting kind of sick of him always talking about my fateful night.

I'd been sorry about it right away and had gotten sorrier about it ever since, and was now so sorry about it that him rubbing it in my face did not make me one bit sorrier, it just made me think of him as being kind of a dick.

"Can I go to bed now?" I said.

"Not yet," Abnesti said. "It is hours to go before you sleep."

Then he sent me into Small Workroom 3, where some dude I didn't know was sitting.

V

"Rogan," the dude said.

"Jeff," I said.

"What's up?" he said.

"Not much," I said.

We sat tensely for a long time, not talking.

I kept waiting to feel myself all of a sudden wanting to jump Rogan's bones.

But no.

Maybe ten minutes passed.

We got some rough customers in here. I noted that Rogan had a tattoo of a rat on his neck, a rat that had just been knifed and was crying. But even through its tears it was knifing a smaller rat, who just looked surprised.

Finally Abnesti came on the P.A.

"That's it, guys, thanks," he said.

"What the fuck was that about?" Rogan said.

Good question, Rogan, I thought. Why had we been left just sitting there? In the same manner that Heather and Rachel had been left just sitting there? Then I had a hunch. To test my hunch, I did a sudden lurch into the Spiderhead. Which Abnesti always made a point of not keeping locked, to show how much he trusted and was unafraid of us.

And guess who was in there?

"Hey, Jeff," Heather said.

"Jeff, get out," Abnesti said.

"Heather, did Mr. Abnesti just now make you decide which of us, me or Rogan, to give some Darkenfloxx™ to?" I said.

"Yes," Heather said. She must have been on some Veri-Talk™, because she spoke the truth in spite of Abnesti's attempt at a withering silencing glance.

"Did you recently fuck Rogan, Heather?" I said. "In addition to me? And also fall in love with him, as you did with me?"

"Yes," she said.

"Heather, honestly," Abnesti said. "Put a sock in it."

Heather looked around for a sock, VeriTalk™ making one quite literal.

Back in my Domain, I did the math: Heather had fucked me three times. Heather had probably also fucked Rogan three times, since, in the name of design consistency, Abnesti would have given Rogan and me equal relative doses of Vivistif™.

And yet, speaking of design consistency, there was still

one shoe to drop, if I knew Abnesti, always a stickler in terms of data symmetry, which was: Wouldn't Abnesti also need Rachel to decide who to Darkenfloxx™, i.e., me or Rogan?

After a short break, my suspicions were confirmed: I found myself again sitting in Small Workroom 3 with Rogan!

Again we sat not talking for a long time. Mostly he picked at the smaller rat and I tried to watch without him seeing.

Then, like before, Abnesti came on the P.A. and said: "That's it, guys, thanks."

"Let me guess," I said. "Rachel's in there with you."

"Jeff, if you don't stop doing that, I swear," Abnesti said.

"And she just declined to Darkenfloxx™ either me or Rogan?" I said.

"Hi, Jeff!" Rachel said. "Hi, Rogan!"

"Rogan," I said. "Did you by any chance fuck Rachel earlier today?"

"Pretty much," said Rogan.

My mind was like reeling. Rachel had fucked me plus Rogan? Heather had fucked me plus Rogan? And everyone who had fucked anyone had fallen in love with that person, then out of it?

What kind of crazy-ass Project Team was this?

I mean, I had been on some crazy-ass Project Teams in my time, such as one where the drip had something in it that made hearing music exquisite, and hence when some Shostakovich was piped in actual bats seemed to circle my Domain, or the one where my legs became totally numb below the waist and yet I found I could still stand fifteen straight hours at a fake cash register, miraculously suddenly able to do extremely hard long-division problems in my mind.

But of all of my crazy-ass Project Teams this was by far the most crazy-assed.

I could not help but wonder what tomorrow would bring.

VI

Except today wasn't even over.

I was again called into Small Workroom 3. And was sitting there when this unfamiliar guy came in.

"I'm Keith!" he said, rushing over to shake my hand.

He was a tall Southern drink of water, all teeth and wavy hair.

"Jeff," I said.

"Really nice meeting you!" he said.

Then we sat there not talking. Whenever I looked over at Keith, he would gleam his teeth at me and shake his head all wry, as if to say, "Odd job of work, isn't it?"

"Keith," I said. "Do you by any chance know two chicks named Rachel and Heather?"

"I sure as heck do," Keith said. And suddenly his teeth had a leering quality to them.

"Did you by any chance have sex with both Rachel and Heather earlier today, three times each?" I said.

"What are you, man, a dang psychic?" Keith said. "You're blowing my mind, I itmit it!"

"Jeff, you're totally doinking with our experimental design integrity," Abnesti said.

"So either Rachel or Heather is sitting in the Spiderhead right now," I said. "Trying to decide."

"Decide what?" Keith said.

"Which of us to Darkenfloxx™," I said.

"Eek," said Keith. And now his teeth looked scared.

"Don't worry," I said. "She won't do it."

"Who won't?" Keith said.

"Whoever's in there," I said.

"That's it, guys, thanks," Abnesti said.

Then, after a short break, Keith and I were once again brought into Small Workroom 3, where once again we waited as either Rachel or Heather declined to Darkenfloxx™ either one of us.

Back in my Domain, I constructed a who-had-fucked-whom chart, which went like this:

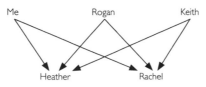

Abnesti came in.

"Despite all your shenanigans," he said, "Rogan and Keith had exactly the same reaction as you did. And as Rachel and Heather did. None of you, at the critical moment, could decide whom to Darkenfloxx™. Which is super. What does that mean? Why is it super? It means that ED289/290 is the real deal. It can make love, it can take love away. I'm almost inclined to start the naming process."

"Those girls did it nine times each today?" I said.

"Peace4All," he said. "LuvInclyned. You seem pissy. Are you pissy?"

"Well, I feel a little jerked around," I said.

"Do you feel jerked around because you still have feelings of love for one of the girls?" he said. "That would need to be noted. Anger? Possessiveness? Residual sexual longing?"

"No," I said.

"You honestly don't feel miffed that a girl for whom you felt love was then funked by two other guys, and, not only that, she then felt exactly the same quality/quantity of love for those guys as she had felt for you, or, in the case of Rachel, was about to feel for you, at the time that she funked Rogan? I think it was Rogan. She may have funked Keith first. Then you, penultimately. I'm vague on the order of operations. I could look it up. But think deeply on this."

I thought deeply on it.

"Nothing," I said.

"Well, it's a lot to sort through," he said. "Luckily it's night. Our day is done. Anything else you want to talk about? Anything else you're feeling?"

"My penis is sore," I said.

"Well, no surprise there," he said. "Think how those girls must feel. I'll send Verlaine in with some cream."

Soon Verlaine came in with some cream.

"Hi, Verlaine," I said.

"Hi, Jeff," he said. "You want to put this on yourself or want me to do it?"

"I'll do it," I said.

"Cool," he said.

And I could tell he meant it.

"Looks painful," he said.

"It really is," I said.

"Must have felt pretty good at the time, though?" he said.

His words seemed to be saying he was envious, but I could see in his eyes, as they looked at my penis, that he wasn't envious at all.

Then I slept the sleep of the dead.

As they say.

VII

Next morning I was still asleep when Abnesti came on the P.A.

"Do you remember yesterday?" he said.

"Yes," I said.

"When I asked which gal you'd like to see on the Darken-floxx™?" he said. "And you said neither?"

"Yes," I said.

"Well, that was good enough for me," he said. "But apparently not good enough for the Protocol Committee. Not good enough for the Three Horsemen of Anality. Come in here. Let's get started—we're going to need to do a kind of Confirmation Trial. Oh, this is going to stink."

I entered the Spiderhead.

Sitting in Small Workroom 2 was Heather.

"So this time," Abnesti said, "per the Protocol Committee, instead of me asking you which girl to give the Darkenfloxx™ to, which the ProtComm felt was too subjective, we're going to give this girl the Darkenfloxx™ no matter what you say. Then see what you say. Like yesterday, we're going to put you on a drip of—Verlaine? Verlaine? Where are you? Are you there? What is it again? Do you have the project order?"

"Verbaluce™, VeriTalk™, ChatEase™," Verlaine said over the P.A.

"Right," Abnesti said. "And did you refresh his Mobi-Pak™? Are his quantities good?"

"I did it," Verlaine said. "I did it while he was sleeping. Plus I already told you I already did it."

"What about her?" Abnesti said. "Did you refresh her MobiPak™? Are her quantities good?"

"You stood right there and watched me, Ray," Verlaine said.

"Jeff, sorry," Abnesti said to me. "We're having a little tension in here today. Not an easy day ahead."

"I don't want you to Darkenfloxx™ Heather," I said.

"Interesting," he said. "Is that because you love her?"

"No," I said. "I don't want you to Darkenfloxx™ anybody."

"I know what you mean," he said. "That is so sweet. Then again: Is this Confirmation Trial about what you want? Not so much. What it's about is us recording what you say as you observe Heather getting Darkenfloxxed™. For five minutes. Five-minute trial. Here we go. Drip on!"

I did not say "Acknowledge."

"You should feel flattered," Abnesti said. "Did we choose Rogan? Keith? No. We deemed your level of speaking more commensurate with our data needs."

I did not say "Acknowledge."

"Why so protective of Heather?" Abnesti said. "One would almost think you loved her."

"No," I said.

"Do you even know her story?" he said. "You don't. You legally can't. Does it involve whiskey, gangs, infanticide? I can't say. Can I imply, somewhat peripherally, that her past, violent and sordid, did not exactly include a dog named Lassie and a lot of family talks about the Bible while Grammy sat doing macramé, adjusting her posture because the quaint fireplace was so sizzling? Can I suggest that, if you knew what I know about Heather's past, making Heather briefly sad, nauseous, and/or horrified might not seem like the worst idea in the world? No, I can't."

"All right, all right," I said.

"You know me," he said. "How many kids do I have?"

"Five," I said.

"What are their names?" he said.

"Mick, Todd, Karen, Lisa, Phoebe," I said.

"Am I a monster?" he said. "Do I remember birthdays around here? When a certain individual got athlete's foot on his groin on a Sunday, did a certain other individual drive over to Rexall and pick up the cream, paying for it with his own personal money?"

That was a nice thing he'd done, but it seemed kind of unprofessional to bring it up now.

"Jeff," Abnesti said. "What do you want me to say here? Do you want me to say that your Fridays are at risk? I can easily say that."

Which was cheap. My Fridays meant a lot to me, and he knew that. Fridays I got to Skype Mom.

"How long do we give you?" Abnesti said.

"Five minutes," I said.

"How about we make it ten?" Abnesti said.

Mom always looked heartsick when our time was up. It had almost killed her when they arrested me. The trial had almost killed her. She'd spent her savings to get me out of real jail and in here. When I was a kid, she'd had long brown hair, past her waist. During the trial she cut it. Then it went gray. Now it was just a white poof about the size of a cap.

"Drip on?" Abnesti said.

"Acknowledge," I said.

"Okay to pep up your language centers?" he said.

"Fine," I said.

"Heather, hello?" he said.

"Good morning!" Heather said.

"Drip on?" he said.

"Acknowledge," Heather said.

Abnesti used his remote.

The Darkenfloxx™ started flowing. Soon Heather was softly crying. Then was up and pacing. Then jaggedly crying. A little hysterical, even.

"I don't like this," she said, in a quaking voice.

Then she threw up in the trash can.

"Speak, Jeff," Abnesti said to me. "Speak a lot, speak in detail. Let's make something useful of this, shall we?"

Everything in my drip felt Grade A. Suddenly I was waxing poetic. I was waxing poetic re what Heather was doing, and waxing poetic re my feelings about what Heather was doing. Basically, what I was feeling was: Every human is born of man and woman. Every human, at birth, is, or at least has the potential to be, beloved of his/her mother/father. Thus every human is worthy of love. As I watched Heather suffer, a great tenderness suffused my body, a tenderness hard to distinguish from a sort of vast existential nausea; to wit, why are such beautiful beloved vessels made slaves to so much pain? Heather presented as a bundle of pain receptors. Heather's mind was fluid, and could be ruined (by pain, by sadness). Why? Why was she made this way? Why so fragile?

Poor child, I was thinking, poor girl. Who loved you? Who loves you?

"Hang in there, Jeff," Abnesti said. "Verlaine! What do you think? Any vestige of romantic love in Jeff's Verbal Commentary?"

"I'd say no," Verlaine said over the P.A. "That's all just pretty much basic human feeling right there."

"Excellent," Abnesti said. "Time remaining?"

"Two minutes," Verlaine said.

I found what happened next very hard to watch. Under the influence of the Verbaluce™, the VeriTalk™, and the ChatEase™, I also found it impossible not to narrate.

In each Workroom was a couch, a desk, and a chair, all, by design, impossible to disassemble. Heather now began disassembling her impossible-to-disassemble chair. Her face was a mask of rage. She drove her head into the wall. Like a wrathful prodigy, Heather, beloved of someone, managed, in her great sadness-fueled rage, to disassemble the chair while continuing to drive her head into the wall.

"Jesus," Verlaine said.

"Verlaine, buck up," Abnesti said. "Jeff, stop crying. Contrary to what you might think, there's not much data in crying. Use your words. Don't make this in vain."

I used my words. I spoke volumes, was precise. I described and redescribed what I was feeling as I watched Heather do what she now began doing, intently, almost beautifully, to her face/head with one of the chair legs.

In his defense, Abnesti was not in such great shape himself: breathing hard, cheeks candy red, as he tapped the screen of his iMac nonstop with a pen, something he did when stressed.

"Time," he finally said, and cut the Darkenfloxx™ off with his remote. "Fuck. Get in there, Verlaine. Hustle it."

Verlaine hustled into Small Workroom 2.

"Talk to me, Sammy," Abnesti said.

Verlaine felt for Heather's pulse, then raised his hands, palms up, so that he looked like Jesus, except shocked instead of beatific, and also he had his glasses up on top of his head.

"Are you *kidding* me?" Abnesti said.

"What now?" Verlaine said. "What do I—"

"Are you fricking *kidding* me?" Abnesti said.

Abnesti burst out of his chair, shoved me out of the way, and flew through the door into Small Workroom 2.

VIII

I returned to my Domain.

At three, Verlaine came on the P.A.

"Jeff," he said. "Please return to the Spiderhead."

I returned to the Spiderhead.

"We're sorry you had to see that, Jeff," Abnesti said.

"That was unexpected," Verlaine said.

"Unexpected plus unfortunate," Abnesti said. "And sorry I shoved you."

"Is she dead?" I said.

"Well, she's not the best," Verlaine said.

"Look, Jeff, these things happen," Abnesti said. "This is science. In science we explore the unknown. It was unknown what five minutes on Darkenfloxx™ would do to Heather. Now we know. The other thing we know, per Verlaine's assessment of your commentary, is that you really, for sure, do not harbor any residual romantic feelings for Heather. That's a big deal, Jeff. A beacon of hope at a sad time for all. Even as Heather was, so to speak, going down to the sea in her ship, you remained totally unwavering in terms of continuing to not romantically love her. My guess is, ProtComm's going to be like: 'Wow, Utica's really leading the pack in terms of providing mind-blowing new data on ED289/290.' "

It was quiet in the Spiderhead.

"Verlaine, go out," Abnesti said. "Go do your bit. Make things ready."

Verlaine went out.

"Do you think I liked that?" Abnesti said.

"You didn't seem to," I said.

"Well, I didn't," Abnesti said. "I hated it. I'm a person. I have feelings. Still, personal sadness aside, that was good.

You did terrific overall. We all did terrific. Heather especially did terrific. I honor her. Let's just—let's see this thing through, shall we? Let's complete it. Complete the next portion of our Confirmation Trial."

Into Small Workroom 4 came Rachel.

IX

"Are we going to Darkenfloxxᵀᴹ Rachel now?" I said.

"Think, Jeff," Abnesti said. "How can we know that you love neither Rachel nor Heather if we only have data regarding your reaction to what just now happened to Heather? Use your noggin. You are not a scientist, but Lord knows you work around scientists all day. Drip on?"

I did not say "Acknowledge."

"What's the problem, Jeff?" Abnesti said.

"I don't want to kill Rachel," I said.

"Well, who does?" Abnesti said. "Do I? Do you, Verlaine?"

"No," Verlaine said over the P.A.

"Jeff, maybe you're overthinking this," Abnesti said. "Is it possible the Darkenfloxx™ will kill Rachel? Sure. We have the Heather precedent. On the other hand, Rachel may be stronger. She seems a little larger."

"She's actually a little smaller," Verlaine said.

"Well, maybe she's tougher," Abnesti said.

"We're going to weight-adjust her dosage," Verlaine said. "So."

"Thanks, Verlaine," Abnesti said. "Thanks for clearing that up."

"Maybe show him the file," Verlaine said.

Abnesti handed me Rachel's file.

Verlaine came back in.

"Read it and weep," he said.

Per Rachel's file, she had stolen jewelry from her mother, a car from her father, cash from her sister, statues from their church. She'd gone to jail for drugs. After four times in jail for drugs, she'd gone to rehab for drugs, then to rehab for prostitution, then to what they call rehab refresh, for people who've been in rehab so many times they are basically immune. But she must have been immune to the rehab refresh, too, because after that came her biggie: a triple murder—her dealer, the dealer's sister, the dealer's sister's boyfriend.

Reading that made me feel a little funny that we'd fucked and I'd loved her.

But I still didn't want to kill her.

"Jeff," Abnesti said. "I know you've done a lot of work on this with Mrs. Lacey. On killing and so forth. But this is not you. This is us."

"It's not even us," Verlaine said. "It's science."

"The mandates of science," Abnesti said. "Plus the dictates."

"Sometimes science sucks," Verlaine said.

"On the one hand, Jeff," Abnesti said, "a few minutes of unpleasantness for Heather—"

"Rachel," Verlaine said.

"A few minutes of unpleasantness for Rachel," Abnesti said, "years of relief for literally tens of thousands of under-loving or overloving folks."

"Do the math, Jeff," Verlaine said.

"Being good in small ways is easy," Abnesti said. "Doing the huge good things, that's harder."

"Drip on?" Verlaine said. "Jeff?"

I did not say "Acknowledge."

"Fuck it, enough," Abnesti said. "Verlaine, what's the name of that one? The one where I give him an order and he obeys it?"

"Docilryde™," Verlaine said.

"Is there Docilryde™ in his MobiPak™?" Abnesti said.

"There's Docilryde™ in every MobiPak™," Verlaine said.

"Does he need to say 'Acknowledge'?" Abnesti said.

"Docilryde™'s a Class C, so—" Verlaine said.

"See, that, to me, makes zero sense," Abnesti said. "What good's an obedience drug if we need his permission to use it?"

"We just need a waiver," Verlaine said.

"How long does that shit take?" Abnesti said.

"We fax Albany, they fax us back," Verlaine said.

"Come on, come on, make haste," Abnesti said, and they went out, leaving me alone in the Spiderhead.

X

It was sad. It gave me a sad, defeated feeling to think that soon they'd be back and would Docilryde™ me, and I'd say "Acknowledge," smiling agreeably the way a person smiles on Docilryde™, and then the Darkenfloxx™ would flow, into Rachel, and I would begin describing, in that rapid, robotic way one describes on Verbaluce™/VeriTalk™/ChatEase™, the things Rachel would, at that time, begin doing to herself.

It was like all I had to do to be a killer again was sit there and wait.

Which was a hard pill to swallow, after my work with Mrs. Lacey.

"Violence finished, anger no more," she'd make me say, over and over. Then she'd have me do a Detailed Remembering re my fateful night.

I was nineteen. Mike Appel was seventeen. We were both wasto. All night he'd been giving me grief. He was smaller, younger, less popular. Then we were out front of Frizzy's, rolling around on the ground. He was quick. He was mean. I was losing. I couldn't believe it. I was bigger, older, yet losing? Around us, watching, was basically everybody we knew. Then he had me on my back. Someone laughed. Someone said, "Shit, poor Jeff." Nearby was a brick. I grabbed it, glanced Mike in the head with it. Then was on top of him.

Mike gave. That is, there on his back, scalp bleeding, he gave, by shooting me a certain look, like: Dude, come on, we're not all that serious about this, are we?

We were.

I was.

I don't even know why I did it.

It was like, with the drinking and the being a kid and the nearly losing, I'd been put on a drip called, like, Temper-Berst or something.

InstaRaje.

LifeRooner.

"Hey, guys, hello!" Rachel said. "What are we up to today?"

There was her fragile head, her undamaged face, one arm lifting a hand to scratch a cheek, legs bouncing with nerves, peasant skirt bouncing, too, clogged feet crossed under the hem.

Soon all that would be just a lump on the floor.

I had to think.

Why were they going to Darkenfloxx™ Rachel? So they could hear me describe it. If I wasn't here to describe it, they wouldn't do it. How could I make it so I wouldn't be here? I could leave. How could I leave? There was only one door out of the Spiderhead, which was autolocked, and on the other side was either Barry or Hans, with that electric wand called the DisciStick™. Could I wait until Abnesti came in, wonk him, try to race past Barry or Hans, make a break for the Main Door?

Any weapons in the Spiderhead? No. Just Abnesti's birthday mug, a pair of running shoes, a roll of breath mints, his remote.

His remote?

What a dope. That was supposed to be on his belt at all times. Otherwise one of us might help ourselves to whatever we found, via Inventory Directory, in our MobiPaks™: some Bonviv™, maybe, some BlissTyme™, some SpeedErUp™.

Some Darkenfloxx™.

Jesus. That was one way to leave.

Scary, though.

Just then, in Small Workroom 4, Rachel, I guess thinking the Spiderhead empty, got up and did this happy little shuffle, like she was some cheerful farmer chick who'd just stepped outside to find the hick she was in love with coming up the road with a calf under his arm or whatever.

Why was she dancing? No reason.

Just alive, I guess.

Time was short.

The remote was well labeled.

Good old Verlaine.

I used it, dropped it down the heat vent, in case I changed my mind, then stood there like: I can't believe I just did that.

My MobiPak™ whirred.

The Darkenfloxx™ flowed.

Then came the horror: worse than I'd ever imagined. Soon my arm was about a mile down the heat vent. Then I was staggering around the Spiderhead, looking for something, anything. In the end, here's how bad it got: I used a corner of the desk.

What's death like?

You're briefly unlimited.

I sailed right out through the roof.

And hovered above it, looking down. Here was Rogan, checking his neck tattoo in the mirror. Here was Keith, squat-thrusting in his underwear. Here was Ned Riley, here was B. Troper, here was Gail Orley, Stefan DeWitt, killers all, all bad, I guess, although, in that instant, I saw it differently. At birth, they'd been charged by God with the responsibility of growing into total fuckups. Had they chosen this? Was it their fault, as they tumbled out of the womb? Had they aspired, covered in placental blood, to grow into harmers, dark forces, life enders? In that first holy instant of breath/awareness (tiny hands clutching and unclutching), had it been their fondest hope to render (via gun, knife, or brick) some innocent family bereft? No; and yet their crooked destinies had lain dormant within them, seeds awaiting water and light to bring forth the most violent, life-poisoning flowers, said water/light actually being the requisite combination of neurological tendency and environmental activation that would transform them (transform us!) into earth's offal, murderers, and foul us with the ultimate, unwashable transgression.

Wow, I thought, was there some Verbaluce™ in that drip or what?

But no.

This was all me now.

I got snagged, found myself stuck on a rooftop gutter, squatted there like an airy gargoyle. I was there but was also everywhere. I could see it all: a clump of leaves in the gutter beneath my see-through foot; Mom, poor Mom, at home in Rochester, scrubbing the shower, trying to cheer herself via thin hopeful humming; a deer near the dumpster, suddenly alert to my spectral presence; Mike Appel's mom, also in Rochester, a bony, distraught check mark occupying a slender strip of Mike's bed; Rachel below in Small Workroom 4, drawn to the one-way mirror by the sounds of my death; Abnesti and Verlaine rushing into the Spiderhead; Verlaine kneeling to begin CPR.

Night was falling. Birds were singing. Birds were, it occurred to me to say, enacting a frantic celebration of day's end. They were manifesting as the earth's bright-colored nerve endings, the sun's descent urging them into activity, filling them individually with life nectar, the life nectar then being passed into the world, out of each beak, in the form of that bird's distinctive song, which was, in turn, an accident of beak shape, throat shape, breast configuration, brain chemistry: some birds blessed in voice, others cursed; some squawking, others rapturous.

From somewhere, something kind asked, *Would you like to go back? It's completely up to you. Your body appears salvageable.*

No, I thought, no thanks, I've had enough.

My only regret was Mom. I hoped someday, in some better place, I'd get a chance to explain it to her, and maybe she'd be proud of me, one last time, after all these years.

From across the woods, as if by common accord, birds left their trees and darted upward. I joined them, flew among them, they did not recognize me as something apart from them, and I was happy, so happy, because for the first time in years, and forevermore, I had not killed, and never would.

EXHORTATION

MEMORANDUM

DATE: *Apr 6*
TO: *Staff*
FROM: *Todd Birnie, Divisional Director*
RE: *March Performance Stats*

I would not like to characterize this as a plea, although it may start to sound like one (!). The fact is, we have a job to do, we have tacitly agreed to do it (did you cash your last paycheck, I know I did, ha ha ha). We have also—to go a step further here—agreed to do the job well. Now we all know that one way to do a job poorly is to be negative about it. Say we need to clean a shelf. Let's use that example. If we spend the hour before the shelf-cleaning talking down the process of cleaning the shelf, complaining about it, dreading it, investigating the moral niceties of cleaning the shelf, whatever, then what happens is, we make the process of cleaning the shelf *more difficult than it really is*. We all know very well that that "shelf" is going to be cleaned, given the current climate, either by you or the guy who replaces you and gets your paycheck, so the question boils down to: Do I want to clean it happy or do I want to clean it sad? Which would be more effective? For me? Which would accomplish my purpose more efficiently? What is my purpose? To get paid. How do I accomplish that purpose most efficiently? I clean that shelf well and clean it quickly. And what mental state helps me clean that shelf well and quickly? Is the answer: Negative? A negative mental state? You know very well that it is not. So the point of this memo is: Positive. The positive mental state will help you clean that shelf well and quickly, thus accomplishing your purpose of getting paid.

What am I saying? Am I saying whistle while you work? Maybe I am. Let us consider lifting a heavy dead carcass such as a whale. (Forgive the shelf/whale thing, we have just come back from our place on Reston Island, where there were 1) a lot of dirty shelves, and 2) yes, believe it or not, an actual dead rotting whale, which Timmy and Vance and I got involved with in terms of the cleanup.) So say you are charged with, you and some of your colleagues, lifting a heavy dead whale carcass onto a flatbed. Now we all know that is hard. And what would be harder is: doing that with a negative attitude. What we found—Timmy and Vance and I—is that even with only a neutral attitude, you are talking a very hard task. We tried to lift that whale while we were just feeling neutral, Timmy and Vance and I, with a dozen or so other folks, and it was a no-go, that whale wouldn't budge, until suddenly one fellow, a former Marine, said that what we needed was some mind over matter, and gathered us in a little circle, and we had a sort of chant. We got "psyched up." We knew, to extend my above analogy, that we had a job to do, and got sort of excited about that, and decided to do it with a positive attitude, and I have to tell you, there was something to that, it was fun, fun when that whale rose into the air, helped by us and some big straps that Marine had in his van, and I have to say that lifting that dead rotting whale onto that flatbed with that group of total strangers was *the high point of our trip.*

So what am I saying? I am saying (and saying it fervently, because it is important): Let's try, if we can, to minimize the grumbling and self-doubt regarding the tasks we must sometimes do around here that maybe aren't on the surface all that pleasant. I'm saying let's try not to dissect every single thing we do in terms of ultimate good/bad/indifferent in terms of morals. The time for that is long past. I hope that each of us had that conversation with ourselves nearly a year ago, when this whole thing started. We have embarked on a path, and having embarked on that path, for the best of reasons (as we decided a year ago), wouldn't it be kind of suicidal to let our progress down that path be impeded by neurotic second-guessing? Have any of you ever swung a sledgehammer? I know that some of you have. I know that some of you did when we took out Rick's patio. Isn't it fun when you don't hold back, but just pound down and down, letting gravity help you? Fellows, what I'm saying is, let gravity help you here, in our workplace situation: Pound down, give in to the natural feelings that I have seen from time to time produce so much great energy in so many of you, in terms of executing your given tasks with vigor and without second-guessing and neurotic thoughts. Remember that record-breaking week Andy had back in October, when he doubled his usual number of units? Regardless of all else, forgetting for the moment all namby-pamby thoughts of right/wrong etc., etc., wasn't that something to see? In and of itself? I think that, if we each look deep down inside of ourselves, weren't we all a little envious? God, he was really pounding down and you could see the energetic joy on his face each time he rushed by us to get additional cleanup towels. And we were all just standing there like, Wow, Andy, what's gotten into you? And no one can argue with his numbers. They are there in our Break Room for all to see, towering above the rest of our numbers, and though Andy has failed to duplicate those numbers in the months since October, 1) no one blames him for that, those were miraculous numbers, and 2) I believe that even if Andy never again duplicates those numbers, he must still, somewhere in his heart, secretly treasure the memory of that magnificent energy flowing out of him that memorable October. I do not honestly think Andy could've had such an October if he had been coddling himself or entertaining any doubtful neurotic thoughts or second-guessing tendencies, do you? I don't. Andy looked totally focused, totally outside himself, you could see it on his face, maybe because of the new baby? (If so, Janice should have a new baby every week, ha ha.)

Anyway, October is how Andy entered a sort of, at least in my mind, de facto Hall of Fame, and is pretty much henceforth excluded from any real close monitoring of his numbers, at least by me. No matter how disconsolate and sort of withdrawn he gets (and I think we've all noticed that he's gotten pretty disconsolate and withdrawn since October), you will not find me closely monitoring his numbers, although as for others I cannot speak, others may be monitoring that troubling falloff in Andy's numbers, although really I hope they're not, that would not be so fair, and believe me, if I get wind of it, I will definitely let Andy know, and if Andy's too depressed to hear me, I'll call Janice at home.

And in terms of why is Andy so disconsolate? My guess is that he's being neurotic, and second-guessing his actions of October—and wow, wouldn't that be a shame, wouldn't that be a no-win, for Andy to have completed that record-breaking October and then sit around boo-hooing about it? Is anything being changed by that boo-hooing? Are the actions Andy did, in terms of the tasks I gave him to do in Room 6, being undone by his boo-hooing, are his numbers on the Break Room wall miraculously scrolling downward, are people suddenly walking out of Room 6 feeling perfectly okay again? Well we all know they are not. No one is walking out of Room 6 feeling perfectly okay. Even you guys, you who do what must be done in Room 6, don't walk out feeling so super-great, I know that, I've certainly done some things in Room 6 that didn't leave me feeling so wonderful, believe me, no one is trying to deny that Room 6 can be a bummer, it is very hard work that we do. But the people above us, who give us our assignments, seem to think that the work we do in Room 6, in addition to being *hard,* is also *important,* which I suspect is why they have begun watching our numbers so closely. And trust me, if you want Room 6 to be an even worse bummer than it already is, then mope about it before, after, and during, then it will really stink, plus, with all the moping, your numbers will go down even further, which guess what: They cannot do. I have been told in no uncertain terms, at the Sectional Meeting, that our numbers are not to go down any further. I said (and this took guts, believe me, given the atmosphere at Sectional): Look, my guys are tired, this is hard work we do, both physically and psychologically. And at that point, at Sectional, believe me, the silence was deafening. And I mean deafening. And the looks I got were not good. And I was reminded, in no uncertain terms, by Hugh Blanchert himself, that our numbers are not to go down. And I was asked to remind you—to remind us, all of us, myself included—that if we are unable to clean our assigned "shelf," not only will someone else be brought in to clean that "shelf," but we ourselves may find ourselves on that "shelf," being that "shelf," with someone else exerting themselves with good positive energy all over us. And at that time I think you can imagine how regretful you would feel, the regret would show in your faces, as we sometimes witness, in Room 6, that regret on the faces of the "shelves" as they are "cleaned," so I am asking you, from the hip, to try your best and not end up a "shelf," which we, your former colleagues, will have no choice but to clean clean clean using all our positive energy, without looking back, in Room 6.

This was all made clear to me at Sectional and now I am trying to make it clear to you.

Well I have gone on and on, but please come by my office, anybody who's having doubts, doubts about what we do, and I will show you pictures of that incredible whale my sons and I lifted with our good positive energy. And of course this information, that is, the information that you are having doubts, and have come to see me in my office, will go no further than my office, although I am sure I do not even have to say that, to any of you, who have known me all these many years.

All will be well and all will be well, etc., etc.,

Todd

AL ROOSTEN

Al Roosten stood waiting behind the paper screen. Was he nervous? Well, he was a little nervous. Although probably a lot less nervous than most people would be. Most people would probably be pissing themselves by now. Was he pissing himself? Not yet. Although, wow, he could understand how someone might actually—

"Let's fire it up!" shouted the MC, a cheerleaderish blonde too old for braids, whose braids were flipping around as for some reason she pretended to jog. "Are we fighting drugs here today or what? Yes we are! Do us businesspeople approve of drugs for our kids? No way, we don't, we're very much against that! Do we use drugs ourselves? Kids, those of you who are here, believe me when I say we don't, and never did! Because, as someone who does feng shui for a living, there's no way I could do my feng shui if I was whacked out on crack, because my business is about discerning energy fields, and if you're cracked up, or on pot, or even if you've had too much coffee, the energy field gets all wonky, believe me, I know, I used to smoke!"

It was a lunchtime auction of Local Celebrities, a Local Celebrity being any sucker dopey enough to answer yes when the Chamber of Commerce asked.

"So that's why we're here raising money for LaffKidsOff-Crack and their antidrug clowns!" the blonde shouted. "Such as Mr. BugOut, who, in his classroom work, with a balloon, makes this thing that starts out as a crack pipe and ends up as a coffin, which I think is so true!"

Larry Donfrey of Larry Donfrey Realty stood nearby in a swimsuit. Donfrey was a good guy. Good but flawed. Not that bright. Always tan. Was Donfrey attractive? Cute? Would the bidders consider Donfrey cuter than him, Al Roosten? Oh, how should he know? Did he like guys? Was he some kind of expert judge on the cuteness of guys?

No, he didn't like guys and never had.

There had been that period in junior high, yes, when he had been somewhat worried that he might perhaps like guys, and had constantly lost in wrestling because, instead of concentrating on his holds he was always mentally assessing whether his thing was hurting inside his cup because he was popping a mild pre-bone or because the tip was sticking out an airhole, and once he was almost sure he'd popped a mild pre-bone when he found his face pressed against Tom Reed's hard abs, which smelled of coconut, but, after practice, obsessing about this in the woods, he realized that he sometimes popped a similar mild pre-bone when the cat sat on his groin in a beam of sun, which proved he didn't have sexual feelings for Tom Reed, since he knew for sure he didn't have sexual feelings for the cat, since he'd never even heard that described as being possible. And from that day on, whenever he found himself wondering whether he liked guys, he always remembered walking exultantly in the woods after the liberating realization that he was no more attracted to guys than to cats, just happily kicking the tops off mushrooms in a spirit of tremendous relief.

A sort of music started up, consisting of a series of loud, thick bumps punctuated by a smattering of feminine groans and something that sounded like a squeaky door, and Larry Donfrey headed down the runway to sudden cheers and whoops.

What the heck? thought Roosten. Whoops? Cheers? Would he get cheers? Whoops? He doubted it. Who whooped/cheered for the round bald guy in the gondolier costume? If he were a woman, he'd cheer/whoop for Donfrey, the guy with the tight ass and ripped brown arms.

The blonde cued Roosten by pointing at him while walking in place.

Oh God oh God.

Roosten stepped warily out from behind the paper screen. No one whooped. He started down the runway. No cheering. The room made the sound a room makes when attempting not to laugh. He tried to smile sexily but his mouth was too dry. Probably his yellow teeth were showing and the place where his gums dipped down.

Frozen in the harsh spotlight, he looked so crazy and old and forlorn and yet residually arrogant that an intense discomfort settled on the room, a discomfort that, in a non-charity situation, might have led to shouted insults or thrown objects but in this case drew a kind of pity whoop from near the salad bar.

Roosten brightened and sent a relieved half wave in the direction of the whoop, and the awkwardness of this gesture—the way it inadvertently revealed how terrified he was—endeared him to the crowd that seconds before had been ready to mock him, and someone else pity-whooped, and Roosten smiled a big loopy grin, which caused a wave of mercy cheers.

Roosten was deaf to the charity in this. What a super level of whoops and cheers. He should do a flex. He would. He did. This caused an increase in the level of whoops and cheers, which, to his ear, were now at least equal in volume to Donfrey's whoops/cheers. Plus Donfrey had been basically naked. Which meant that technically he'd beaten Donfrey, since Donfrey had needed to get naked just to manage a tie with him, Al Roosten.

Ha ha, poor Donfrey! Running around in his skivvies to no avail.

The blonde threw a butterfly net over Roosten's head and he joined Donfrey in the cardboard jail.

Now that he had thrashed Donfrey, he felt a surge of affection for him. Good old Donfrey. He and Donfrey were the twin pillars of the local business community. He didn't know Donfrey well. Just admired him from afar. Just like Donfrey admired him from afar. Once, the whole Donfrey clan had filed into Roosten's shop, Bygone Daze. Donfrey's wife had been beautiful: nice legs, slim back, long hair. You looked at her and couldn't look away. Donfrey's kids had also seemed great, two elflike androgynes politely debating something, possibly the history of the Supreme Court?

Each Celeb had his own barred window in the cardboard jail. Donfrey now stepped away from his and toward Roosten's. How gracious. What a prince. They'd have a little chat. The crowd would jealously wonder what the twin pillars were chatting about in private. But, sorry, no: this was between pillars. Rabble need not apply.

Donfrey was saying something but the music was blaring and Roosten was partly deaf.

Roosten leaned in.

"I said, Don't worry about it, Ed," Donfrey was shouting. "You did fine. Really. No biggie. Give it a week, nobody will even remember it."

What? What the hell? What was Donfrey saying? That he'd done badly? Had embarrassed himself? In front of the whole town? No way. He'd kicked butt. Was Donfrey on some other planet? On drugs? On drugs at an antidrug event? Had Donfrey just called him Ed?

Donfrey could kiss his ass. That fake. That snob. He'd forgotten that. He'd forgotten that Donfrey was a snobby fake. That time the Donfreys came into Bygone Daze, they'd immediately turned and walked out, as if they'd found Roosten's vintage collectibles too dusty and ill-selected for the Donfrey house, a literal mansion on a hill. And Donfrey's wife wasn't beautiful, Roosten suddenly honestly admitted; she was pale. A pale, haughty waif. As far as Donfrey's kids—if those kids belonged to him? He'd scruff them up a bit. Try and de-elfify them. Were they girls or boys? You honestly couldn't tell.

He didn't have kids himself. Had never married. He had the boys, however. The boys were his nephews. The boys were not elfin. *Au contraire*. The boys were whatever was the opposite of elfin. Trollish? Clodhoppers? No, the boys were great. The boys were all-boy. And how. Possibly too much so. Why his sister, Mag, insisted on taking them to Budgi-Cutz when Budgi-Cutz made them look like three hulking versions of the same odd Germanic roundhead, their bangs cut straight across, he did not know. Every night was a three-way grunting/wrestling fest in the basement, the boys calling one another Skuzzknuckles or FartIngestron until one of them bonked his round head into something metal and they all helped the hurt one upstairs, tears running down their wrestling-engorged cheeks, like three suddenly repentant Nazis—

Not Nazis. Jeez. Germans. Energetic prewar Germanic lads. Healthy young Beethovens. Although as far as Beethoven, he doubted Beethoven had ever pried a prayer-book rack off the pew with his bare hands on a dare from another Beethoven, while a third Beethoven proudly displayed, on a hymnal, four tightly rolled snot towers he'd just—

It was the divorce. The divorce had made the boys wild. It was sad about Mag. In high school, Al had been the popular wrestler and Mag had been the stout girl in ChristLife with a big crush on Christ. They'd lived on their parents' farm. But somehow only Mag had turned out farmish. Junior year, she'd started dating Ken Glenn, equally agrarian, with plate-sized ears. There'd been jokes at the time about Mag and Ken being married in overalls. There'd been jokes about Mag and Ken being married in a church full of barnyard animals. If there was ever a marriage you'd expect to last, this one was it: two homely Christian farmers. But no, Ken had left Mag for another farmer's—

Mag was not homely. She was simple, she had a kind of simple earthy—

She was handsome. A handsome woman. She—everything was where it should be. She carried herself well. Except when bellowing at the boys. Then her face became a red contorted mask. You saw her frustration at being the only divorced woman in her extremely strict church, her embarrassment at having had to move in with her brother, her worry that, if he lost the shop (as it now appeared almost certain he would), she'd have to quit school and get a third job. Last night he'd found her at the kitchen table after her shift at Costco, fast asleep across her community-college nursing text. A nurse at forty-five. That was a laugh. He found that laughable. Although he didn't find it laughable. He found it admirable. A snob like Donfrey might find it laughable. A snob like Donfrey would take one look at Mag in her baggy nurse's outfit and hustle his spoiled elves back to the stupendous Donfrey mansion, which had recently been featured in the Lifestyles section of the—

Oh, mansion shmansion. Did Gandhi's house have the largest outdoor trampoline in the tristate area? Did Jesus have a two-acre remote-controlled car track, with mountains to scale and a little village that lit up at night?

Not in his Bible.

Huh. The cardboard jail was now filled with Celebs. How had that happened? He'd apparently missed the runway walks of Max of Max's Auto, Ed Berden of Steak-n-Roll, and the freakishly tall twin hippie brothers who ran Coffee-Minded.

The blonde was standing silently now, head down, as if waiting for her experience-based profundity to overflow into the show-stopping heartfelt speech that would establish her once and for all as the most pain-racked person in the place.

"Folks, we've arrived at our most important aspect," she said softly. "Which is our auction. Which is to be silent. Without you folks, you know what? LaffKidsOffCrack is just some guys with strong antidrug feelings, wearing weird clothes in their own homes. Write down your bid, someone will come around. Later, if you are the one who won, you'll be taken to lunch by your Celebrity who you bid for."

Was it over?

It appeared to be over.

Could he sneak out?

He could if he bent low.

He bent low and booked it as the blonde droned on.

In the changing area, he found Donfrey's clothes slopped over a chair: expensive pleated pants, nice silk shirt. On the floor were Donfrey's keys and wallet

Just like Donfrey to junk up a perfectly nice changing area.

Oh, why be mad at Donfrey? Donfrey hadn't done anything to him. He'd just made a comment, trying to be nice. Trying to be charitable. To someone beneath him.

Roosten took a step forward and gave the wallet a kick. Wow, did it ever slide. Right under a stack of risers. Like a hockey puck. There were the keys, alone now, underscoring the absence of the wallet. Yikes. He could say he'd accidentally kicked the wallet under there. Which was sort of true. He hadn't thought about it, really. He'd just felt like kicking it and then he had. He was impulsive like that. That was one of the good things about him. It was how he'd bought the shop. Failing shop. He gave the keys a kick. What the hell? Why had he done that? They slid even better than the wallet. Now wallet and keys were far under the risers.

Gosh, too bad. Too bad he'd accidentally kicked those things under there.

Donfrey burst into the changing area, talking loudly on his cell in a know-it-all voice.

She was fine, Donfrey was bellowing. Nervous but psyched. Being brave. Stiff upper lip. Kid was solid gold. Always did her share: carried the laundry down on her day, dragged the trash to the street. Hadn't slept all week. Too excited. What she was looking forward to most? Running with her class in gym. Imagine: all your life you're limping around with a bent-in foot, then they finally figure out a way to fix it. It was scary, yes, Jesus, the brace literally broke and reformed the foot. Poor thing had been waiting so long. They had to haul ass pronto, pick her up, shoot over to the place. They were running late, the auction thing had gone on and on. He probably should've skipped it, but it was such a terrific cause.

Roosten finished dressing quickly and left the changing area.

Jeez, what was all that about? Apparently, one of the elves wasn't as perfect as she—

Had one of the elves had a limp? He couldn't remember.

Well, that was sad. The sickness of a kid was—children were the future. He'd do anything to help that kid. If one of the boys had a bent foot, he'd move heaven and earth to get it fixed. He'd rob a bank. And if the boy was a girl, even worse. Who'd ask a clubfoot or bentfoot or whatever to dance? There your daughter sat, with her crutch, all dressed up, not dancing.

Hundreds of dry leaf fragments were skittering across the FlapJackers parking lot. A bird on a parking bumper bolted, alarmed at the advance of the leaves. Stupid leaves, they'd never catch that bird.

Unless he killed it with a stone, left it lying there. They'd be so grateful they'd declare him King of Leaves.

Ha ha.

He gave a pile of leaves a vicious kick.

Shit. He felt like crying. Why, what was it, what was making him so sad?

Off he drove through the town where he'd lived his whole life. The river was high. The grade school had a new bike rack. A ton of dogs leaped to the fence as usual as he passed the Flannery Kennel. Next to the kennel was Mike's Gyros. Once, during that terrible seventh-grade year, Mom had taken him to Mike's for a Coke.

"What seems to be the problem, Al?" Mom had said.

"Everyone's calling me bossy and fat," he'd said. "Plus they say I'm sneaky."

"Well, Al," she'd said, "you are bossy, you are fat. And I'm guessing you can be pretty sneaky. But you know what else you are? You have what is called moral courage. When you know something is right, you do it, no matter what the cost."

Mom could sometimes be full of it. Once, she'd said she could tell by the way he ran upstairs that he'd make a great mountain climber. Once, when he managed a B-minus in math, she'd said he should be an astronomer.

Good old Mom. She'd always made him feel special.

Suddenly his face was hot. He felt Mom looking at him from Heaven, sternly but wryly, in that way she'd had, as if saying, Hello, are we maybe forgetting something?

Well, it had been an accident. He had just accidentally misplaced some things inadvertently. With his foot. Via spontaneously kicking them erroneously.

Mom's eyes narrowed in Heaven.

They were being mean to me, he said.

Mom in Heaven tapped her foot.

What was he supposed to do? Go racing back, lead them to the keys? They'd know he'd done it. Plus Donfrey was probably long gone. Probably Donfrey's wife had a set of spare keys. Although Donfrey's wife hadn't been there. Well, someone could drive Donfrey home. After he'd fruitlessly looked for his keys awhile. Causing him to be so late, they'd have to reschedule the kid's—

Shit.

Oh, they'd live. No one was dying from this. So a kid had to wait a few more months for her—

Roosten pulled into a white-stoned driveway. He had to think. A Yorkie rushed up to the fence, barking ceremonially. Then a chicken came up. Huh. A chicken and a Yorkie, living in the same yard. They stood side by side, looking at Roosten.

Eureka.

He saw how he could do it.

He'd sneak back, pretend he'd never left. Everyone would be searching for the wallet and keys. He'd look alongside them awhile. When they were about to give up, he'd say, I assume you've already looked under those risers?

Uh, well, no, Donfrey would say.

Might be worth a try, Roosten would suggest.

They'd get some guys and move the risers. And there would be the wallet and there would be the keys.

Wow, Donfrey would say. You are amazing.

Just a hunch, Roosten would say. I simply mentally eliminated all other possible options.

I'm afraid I've underestimated you, Donfrey would say. We have to have you over to the house soon.

To the mansion? Roosten would say.

And Al? Donfrey would say. Sorry about that time we walked out of your shop. That was rude. And Al? Sorry I called you Ed earlier.

Oh, did you? Roosten would say. I didn't even really notice.

Dinner at the mansion would go well. Soon he'd basically be part of the family. He'd just drop by whenever. That would be nice. Nice to hang out in a mansion. Sometimes the boys might come along. Although the boys had better not break anything. They'd have to wrestle outside. One thing he did not need was his friends' mansion trashed. He saw Donfrey's gorgeous wife, distressed by all the things the boys had broken, collapse into a chair and start weeping.

Thanks, boys, great, thanks a lot for that. Go outside. Go outside and sit quietly.

Now the moon is full in the big window and he and Donfrey are wearing tuxes and Donfrey's wife is wearing something low-cut and golden.

This dinner is great, he says. All your dinners have been so great.

It's the least we could do, says Donfrey. You helped us out so much that time I stupidly lost my keys.

Ha ha, yes, well, about that? Roosten says.

Then he tells them all about it: how he did an unfortunate thing, saw the light, raced back to help.

What a riot! says Donfrey.

That took guts, says Donfrey's wife. Coming back like that.

I'd say it took moral courage, says Donfrey.

Your honesty actually makes us admire you all the more, says Donfrey's wife.

Mag was there, too. What was she doing there? Well, it was fine, she could stay. Mag was a good egg. Decent conversationalist. The Donfreys would appreciate her good qualities. Just like they appreciated his good qualities. And wouldn't Mom love seeing that, her kids finally getting their due from some sophisticated people in a beautiful mansion.

An odd inadvertent sound of contentment jerked Roosten out of his reverie.

Ha.

What the hell. Where was he?

The Yorkie was sniffing the chicken. The chicken didn't seem to mind. Or notice. The chicken had a laserlike focus on him, Al Roosten.

Yeah, right. Like any of that was happening. Like he was racing back. They'd see through him. They'd fry his ass. People were always seeing through him and frying his ass. When he'd stolen Kirk Desner's flip-downs, the kids on the team had seen through him and fried his ass. The time he'd cheated on Syl, Syl had seen through him, broken off their engagement, and cheated on him with Charles, which had fried his ass possibly worse than any single other ass frying he'd ever had, in a life that, it recently seemed, was simply a series of escalating ass fries.

He turned his mind toward Mom, as always, for a word of encouragement.

What, that Donfrey doofus never made a mistake in his life? Mom said. Was never inadvertently involved in something unfortunate that sadly occurred? And now wants to label you a dick, or scum, or a bad immature person, because of one small mistake? Does that seem fair? Don't you think he's probably needed forgiveness sometime in his life?

Probably, Roosten said.

Oh, definitely, Mom said. I've known you all your life, Al, and there's not a mean bone in your body. You are Al Roosten. Don't forget that. Sometimes you think something's wrong with you, but every time, turns out, there isn't.

Why beat yourself up about this and, in so doing, miss the beauty of the actual moment?

The lilt of Mom's voice in his head cheered him.

He pulled out of the driveway. Mom was right. The world was beautiful. Here was the pioneer graveyard with its leaning yellowed stones. Here was the very vivid Jiffy Lube. A dense ball of birds went linear, then settled into the branches of a lightning-blasted tree. He knew it wasn't really Mom in his head. He was just imagining what Mom would have said. Who knew what Mom would have said? She could be a crazy old broad there at the end. But he sure did miss her.

He thought again of the crippled girl. They'd missed the appointment and had to reschedule. The only available slot was months away. In the dark of night, she reached down for her bent foot and let out a groan. She'd been so close, so close to getting—

That was crap. That was negative. You had to let the healing begin. Everyone knew that. You had to love yourself. What was positive? The shop: thinking up ways to improve it, make it halfway decent, bring it back to life. He'd put in a coffee bar. Tear out that old stained rug. There, he was feeling better already. You had to have joy. Joy kept a guy going. Once he got the shop viable, he'd go beyond that, make it great. Lines of people would be waiting when he arrived every morning. As he pushed his way through the crowd in his mind, everyone seemed to be asking, with smiles and pats on his back, would he consider running for mayor? Would he do for the town what he'd done for Bygone Daze?

Ha ha, what a fun deal that would be, running for mayor. What colors would his banners be? What was his slogan?

AL ROOSTEN, FRIEND TO ALL.

That was good.

AL ROOSTEN, THE BEST AMONG US.

Little vain.

AL ROOSTEN: LIKE YOU, ONLY BETTER.

Ha ha.

Here was the shop. Nobody was waiting to get in. A muddy tarp had blown over from the junkyard and plastered itself against the window. Across from the junkyard was the viaduct where the hoboes hung out. Those hoboes were ruining his—

He believed they preferred to be called "homeless." Hadn't he read that? "Hobo" being derogatory? Jesus, that took nerve. Guy never works a day in his life, just goes around stealing pies off windowsills, then starts yelping about his rights? He'd like to walk up to a homeless and call him a hobo. He'd do it too, he would, he'd grab that damn hobo by the collar and go, Hey, hobo, you're ruining my business. I've missed my rent two months in a row. Go back to the foreign country you probably—

He just really hated those beggars walking past his shop with their crude signs. Couldn't they at least spell right? Yesterday one had walked by with a sign that said, PLEASE HELP HOMLESS. He'd felt like shouting, Hey, sorry you lost your hom! They spent enough time under that viaduct, couldn't they at least proofread each other's—

As he parked the car, his mind went strangely blank. Where was he? The shop. Ugh. Where were his keys? On the same old ugly lanyard, impossible to get out of your pocket.

Jesus, he couldn't stand the thought of going in.

He'd sit there alone all afternoon. Why did he have to do it? For what? For who?

Mag. Mag and the boys were counting on him.

He sat a minute, breathing deeply.

An old man in filthy clothes staggered up the street, dragging a cardboard square on which, no doubt, he slept. His teeth were ghoulish, his eyes wet and red. Roosten imagined himself leaping from the car, knocking the man to the ground, kicking him and kicking him, teaching him, in this way, a valuable lesson on how to behave.

The man gave Roosten a weak smile, and Roosten gave the man a weak smile back.

THE SEMPLICA GIRL DIARIES

(September 3)

Having just turned 40 have resolved to embark on grand
project of writing every day in this new black book just got at
OfficeMax. Exciting to think how in one year, at rate of one
page/day, will have written 365 pages, and what a picture of
life and times then available for kids & grandkids, even
greatgrandkids, whoever, all are welcome (!) to see how life
really was/is now. Because what do we know of other times
really? How clothes smelled and carriages sounded? Will future people know, for example, about sound of airplanes
going over at night, since airplanes by that time passé? Will
future people know sometimes cats fought in night? Because

by that time some chemical invented to make cats not fight? Last night dreamed of two demons having sex and found it was only two cats fighting outside window. Will future people be aware of concept of "demons"? Will they find our belief in "demons" quaint? Will "windows" even exist? Interesting to future generations that even sophisticated college grad like me sometimes woke in cold sweat, thinking of demons, believing one possibly under bed? Anyway, what the heck, am not planning on writing encyclopedia, if any future person is reading this, if you want to know what a "demon" was, go look it up, in something called an encyclopedia, if you even still have those!

Am getting off track, due to tired, due to those fighting cats.

Will write twenty minutes a night, no matter how tired.

So goodnight to all future generations. Please know I was a person like you, I too breathed air and tensed legs while trying to sleep and, when writing with pencil, sometimes brought pencil to nose to smell. Although who knows, maybe you future people write with laser pens? But probably even those have a certain smell? Do future people still sniff their (laser) pens? Well, it is getting late and I am going far afield in these philosophical speculations. But hereby resolve to write in this book at least twenty minutes a night. (If discouraged, just think of how much will have been recorded for posterity after one mere year!)

———

(September 5)

Oops. Missed a day. Things hectic. Will summarize yesterday. Yesterday a bit rough. While picking kids up at school, bumper fell off Park Avenue. Note to future generations: "Park Avenue" = type of car. Ours not new. Ours oldish. Bit rusty. Eva got in, asked what was meaning of "junkorama." At that moment, bumper fell off. Mr. Renn, history teacher, quite helpful, retrieved bumper (note: write letter of commendation to principal), saying he too once had car whose bumper fell off, when poor, in college. Eva assured me it was all right bumper had fallen off. I replied of course it was all right, why wouldn't it be all right, it was just something that had happened, I certainly hadn't caused. Image that stays in mind is of three sweet kids in backseat, sad chastened expressions on little faces, timidly holding bumper across laps. One end of bumper had to hang out Eva's window and today she has sniffles, plus small cut on hand from place where bumper was sharp. Mr. Renn attached hankie to end of bumper hanging out window. When Eva worried aloud about us forgetting to return hankie ("Well, Daddy, we are the careless kind"), I said I hardly saw us as careless kind. Then of course, on way home, hankie blew off.

Lilly, as always, put all in perspective, by saying who cares about stupid bumper, we're going to get a new car soon anyway, when rich, right? Upon arriving home, put bumper in garage. In garage, found dead large mouse or small squirrel crawling with maggots. Used shovel to transfer majority of squirrel/mouse to Hefty bag. Smudge or stain of squirrel/ mouse remains on garage floor, like oil stain w/embedded fur tufts.

Stood looking up at house, sad. Thought: Why sad? Don't be sad. If sad, will make everyone sad. Went in happy, not mentioning bumper, squirrel/mouse smudge, maggots, then gave Eva extra ice cream due to I had spoken harshly to her.

She is sweetest kid. Biggest heart. Once, when little, found dead bird in yard and placed on swingset slide, so it could "see him fambly." Cried when we threw out old rocking chair, claiming it had told her it wanted to live out rest of life in basement.

Have to do better! Be kinder. Start now. Soon they will be grown and how sad, if only memory of you is testy stressed guy in bad car.

Must Do List: Balance checkbook. Get inspection sticker for Park Ave. Replace bumper. (Note to self: bumper replacement necessary for inspection sticker?) Scrub squirrel/ mouse smudge so kids can do summer plays in garage.

Should Do List: Clean basement. (Recent rain caused mini-flood, which ruined boxes/shipping materials stockpiled for Xmas. Also, guinea pig cage was like floating around. Moved to top of washer. Now, when doing laundry, must move cage temporarily back into water.)

When will I have sufficient leisure/wealth to sit on haybale watching moon rise, while in luxurious mansion family sleeps? At that time, will have chance to reflect deeply on meaning of life etc., etc. Have a feeling and have always had a feeling that this and other good things will happen for us!

(Sept. 6)

Very depressing birthday party today at home of Lilly's friend Leslie Torrini.

House is mansion where Lafayette once stayed. Torrinis showed us Lafayette's room: now their "Fun Den." Plasma TV, pinball game, foot massager. Thirty acres, six outbuildings (they call them "outbuildings"): one for Ferraris (three), one for Porsches (two, plus one he is rebuilding), one for historical merry-go-round they are restoring as family (!). Across trout-stocked stream, red Oriental bridge flown in from China. Showed us hoofmark from some dynasty. In front room, near Steinway, plaster cast of hoofmark from even earlier dynasty, in wood of different bridge. Picasso autograph, Disney autograph, dress Greta Garbo once wore, all displayed in massive mahogany cabinet.

Vegetable garden tended by guy named Karl.

Lilly: Wow, this garden is like ten times bigger than our whole yard.

Flower garden, tended by separate guy, weirdly also named Karl.

Lilly: Wouldn't you love to live here?

Me: Lilly, ha ha, don't ah . . .

Pam (my wife, very sweet, love of life!): What, what is she

saying wrong, wouldn't you? Wouldn't you love to live here? I know I would.

In front of house, on sweeping lawn, largest SG arrangement ever seen, all in white, white smocks blowing in breeze, and Lilly says: Can we go closer?

Leslie, her friend: We can but we don't, usually.

Leslie's mother, dressed in Indonesian sarong: We don't, as we already have, many times, dear, but you perhaps would like to? Perhaps this is all very new and exciting to you?

Lilly, shyly: It is, yes.

Leslie's mom: Please, go, enjoy.

Lilly races away.

Leslie's mom, to Eva: And you dear?

Eva stands timidly against my leg, shakes head no.

Just then father (Emmett) appears, holding freshly painted leg from merry-go-round horse, says time for dinner, hopes we like sailfish flown in fresh from Guatemala, prepared with a rare spice found only in one tiny region of Burma, which had to be bribed out, and also he had to design and build a special freshness-ensuring container for the sailfish.

The kids can eat later, in the treehouse, says Leslie's mom. We bought special table settings. The ones we previously had in the treehouse were Russian, from when we lived there. Very nice but sort of worn. Also, the candleholders were ancient. I am talking ancient as in Romanov ancient.

And last week we finally got cable run up there, says Emmett.

He indicates the treehouse, which is painted Victorian and has a gabled roof and a telescope sticking out and what looks like a small solar panel.

Thomas: Wow, that treehouse is like twice the size of our actual house.

Pam (whispering): Don't say "like."

Me: Oh, ha ha, let him say what he wants, let's not be—

Thomas: That treehouse is twice the size of our actual house.

(Thomas, as usual, exaggerating: treehouse not twice size of our house. Is more like one-third size of our house. Still, yes: big treehouse.)

Our present not the very worst. Although possibly least expensive (someone brought a mini–DVD player, someone brought a lock of hair from an actual mummy(!)), it was, in my opinion, the most heartfelt. Because Leslie (who appeared disappointed at the lock of mummy hair, and said so, because she already had one (!)), was, it seemed to me, touched by the simplicity of our paper doll set. And although we did not view it as kitsch at the time we bought it, when Leslie's mom said, Les, check it out, kitsch or what, don't you love it? I thought: Yes, well, maybe it is kitsch, maybe we did intend. In any event, this eased the blow when the next present was a ticket to the Preakness (!), as Leslie has recently become interested in horses, and has begun getting up early to feed their nine horses, whereas previously she had categorically refused to feed the six llamas.

Leslie's mom: So guess who ended up feeding the llamas?

Leslie (sharply): Mom, don't you remember back then I always had yoga?

Leslie's mom: Although actually, honestly? It was a blessing, a chance for me to rediscover what terrific animals they are, after school, on days on which Les had yoga.

Leslie: Like every day, yoga?

Leslie's mom: I guess you just have to trust your kids, trust that their innate interest in life will win out in the end, don't you think? Which is what is happening now, with Les and horses. God she loves them.

Leslie: They're wonderful.

Pam: Our kids, we can't even get them to pick up what Ferber does in the front yard.

Leslie's mom: And Ferber is?

Me: Dog.

Leslie's mom: Ha ha yes, well, everything poops, isn't that just *it*?

Though is true we cannot keep yard picked up, even with recent attempt at schedule, did not like Pam sharing this with world, as if our kids, in addition to less nicely dressed than Leslie, also less responsible, as if dog not perfectly good pet relative to llama, horse, parrot (parrot in upstairs hall says "Bonne nuit!" as I pass to pee) etc., etc.

After dinner, strolled grounds with Emmett, who is surgeon, does something two days a week with brain-inserts, small electronic devices? Or possibly biotronic? They are very small. Hundreds can fit on head of pin? Or dime? Did not totally follow. Asked about my work, I told. He said

well, huh, amazing the strange arcane things our culture re-
quires some of us to do, degrading things, things that offer
no tangible benefit to anyone, how do they expect people to
continue to even hold their heads up?

Could not think of response. Note to self: Think up response, send on card, thus striking up friendship with Emmett?

Returned to house, sat on special star-watching platform
as stars came out. Our kids sat watching stars fascinated, as
if no stars in our neighborhood. What, I said, no stars in our
neighborhood? No response. From anyone. Actually, stars
there did seem brighter. On star platform, had too much to
drink, and suddenly everything I thought of seemed stupid.
So just went quiet, like in stupor.

Pam drove home, I sat sullen and drunk in passenger seat
of Park Ave. Kids babbling about what a great party it was,
Lilly especially. Thomas spouting all these boring llama facts
per Emmett.

Lilly: I can't wait till my party. My party is two weeks,
right?

Pam: What do you want to do for your party, sweetie?

Long silence in car.

Lilly, finally, sadly: Oh, I don't know. Nothing, I guess.

Pulled up to house. Another silence as we regarded blank
empty yard. That is, mostly crabgrass and no red Oriental
bridge w/ancient hoofprints and no outbuildings and not a
single SG, but only Ferber, who we'd kind of forgotten about,
and who, as usual, had circled round and round the tree

until nearly choking to death on his gradually shortening leash, having basically tethered himself to the ground in supine position, and was looking up at us with begging eyes in which desperation was combined with a sort of low boiling anger.

Let him off leash, he shot me hostile look, took dump extremely close to porch.

Watched to see if kids would take initiative and pick up. But no. Kids only slumped past and stood exhausted by front door. Then I knew I should take initiative and pick up. But was tired and knew I had to come in and write in this stupid book.

Do not really like rich people, as they make us poor people feel dopey and inadequate. Not that we are poor. I would say we are middle. We are very very lucky. I know that. But still, it is not right that rich people make us middle people feel dopey and inadequate.

Am writing this still drunk and it is getting late and tomorrow is Monday, which means work.

Work work work. Stupid work. Am so tired of work.

Goodnight.

(Sept. 7)

Just reread that last entry and should clarify.

Am not tired of work. It is a privilege to work. I do not hate the rich. I aspire to be rich myself. And when we finally do get our own bridge, trout, treehouse, SGs, etc., at least will know we really earned them, unlike, say, the Torrinis, who, I feel, must have family money.

Today at work, at lunch, was Fall Fling. Down we all went, perhaps a thousand folks streaming out. Little trio playing. Someone had distributed orange and yellow mini-flags stamped "FF," which soon nearly covered ground. Fake river runs through courtyard, many assholes had dropped their mini-flags into fake river. Filtering device at one end soon clogged with mini-flags, maintenance man with several mini-flags sticking out of rear pocket crossly going around attempting to dislodge mini-flags from filter with yardstick.

As always they served these flat little dry sandwiches. By time our group got down, many sandwiches already on ground around serving table, with heel marks.

Threw ourselves down on berm, ate hurriedly.

Sat thinking of Eva. Such a sweetie. Last night, after party, found her sad in her room. Asked why. She said no reason. But in sketchpad: crayon pic of row of sad SGs. Could tell were meant to be sad due to frowns went down off faces like Fu Manchus and tears were dropping in arcs, flowers springing up where tears hit ground. Note to self: talk to her, explain it does not hurt, they are not sad, but actually happy, given what their prior conditions were like: they chose, are glad, etc.

Very moving piece on NPR re. Bangladeshi SG sending money home: hence her parents able to build small shack. (Note to self: Find online, download, play for Eva. First fix computer. Computer superslow. Due to low memory? Possibly delete "CircusLoser"? Acrobats run all jerky, due to low memory + elephants do not hop = no fun.)

Soon was nearly one, we returned to work. In elevator, some still holding our little dry sandwiches, stood all of us red-faced men in ties, making jokes about enough Fall Flinging, the Fall Fling has been Flung, etc., etc. Then the embarrassed silence as we, in our minds, resaid the things we had just enthusiastically heatedly said, as if vying for some sort of Stupid Utterance Prize.

Then brief period during which we each surreptitiously cut eyes up at mirrored ceiling of elevator to check bald spots etc., etc., see what we looked like "from above."

Anders said: I must appear pretty weird to birds.

No one laughed, all just made that sound that is like laugh placeholder, so Anders wouldn't feel bad, as his mother has recently passed away.

(Sept. 8)

Just now returned from long walk in Woodcliffe.

All over up there, men my age reading in big chairs under orange affluent lights. Where is my big chair? Orange light? No big chair, no affluent lights, no book-lined room. Why is art on our walls so lame? We have only one of old-time cars got at Target and one of generic beach w/Ferris wheel, from garage sale. What are we doing wrong here? Where our expensive framed original art, signed by artist? (Note to self: Befriend young artist? Young artist comes to house, is so impressed with family, paints portrait of family gratis? Still, expensive to frame. Maybe artist so impressed with family, frames it himself, i.e., frame = part of gift?) In Woodcliffe, everything lavish. Beautiful flowerbeds, night-time smell of cedar mulch, speedboats on lawns in moonlight. Behind big turreted house on corner of Longfellow + Purdy Way, yard slopes down to 200 yards of perfect grass. There in the dark, fifteen (I counted) SGs hanging silently, white smocks in moonlight. Breathtaking. Wind picks up, they go off at slight angle, smocks and hair (long, flowing, black) assuming same angle. Incredible flowers (tulips, roses, something bright orange, long stalky things of white clusters) shaking in wind with paper-on-paper sound. From inside, flute music. Makes one think of ancient times and affluent men of those times building great gardens, roaming through while holding forth on philosophy, bounty of earth having been lassoed for the pleasure of etc., etc.

Wind stops, everything returns to vertical. From across lawn: soft sighing, smattering of mumbled foreign phrases. Perhaps saying goodnight? Perhaps saying, in own lingo, gosh that was some strong wind?

Almost went down for closer look, possible conversation, but at last minute caught myself, thought: Wait, no, trespassing, bad idea.

Stood awhile watching, thinking, praying: Lord, give us more. Give us enough. Help us not fall behind peers. Help us not, that is, fall further behind peers. For kids' sake. Do not want them scarred by how far behind we are.

That is all I ask.

Dog started barking, dashed out between two SGs, one of whom let out little shriek. But dog on lead. Snapped back. From house: Calm down, Brownie! Brownie, mellow! Heard this from tree-shadow, hurried away.

(Sept. 12)

Nine days to Lilly's b-day. Kind of dread this. Too much pressure. Do not want to have bad party. Why issue? Possibly own thirteenth b-day party? Horseback riding and Ken Dryzniak nearly paralyzed in fall? Plus cake was stale. Snake menaced Kate Fresslen. Dad killed snake with hoe, bits of snake flew up, soiling Kate's dress? Or maybe this b-day stress perfectly normal, all parents feel?

Had asked Lilly for list of b-day gift ideas. Today came home to envelope labeled POSSIBLE GIFT LIST. Inside, clippings from some catalog: *"Resting Fierceness." A pair of fierce Porcelain jungle cats are tamed (at least for now!) on highly detailed ornamental pillows, but their wildness is not to be underestimated. Left-Facing Cheetah: $350. Right-Facing Tiger: $325.* Then on Post-It: DAD, SECOND CHOICE: *"Girl Reading to Little Sister"* figurine: *This childhood study by Nevada artist Dani will recall in porcelain the joys of "story time" and the tender moments shared by all. Girl and little girl reading on polished rock: $280.*

Discouraging, I felt. Because 1) Why does young girl of twelve want such old-lady gift, and 2) Where does girl of twelve get idea that $300 = appropriate amount for b-day gift? For us it was one shirt, one shirt we didn't want, usually homemade. Once got basketball but was overly bouncy ABA type, red, white, and blue, with, for some reason, drawing of clown on it. When bounced, went like two feet higher than normal ball. Friends called it my "bouncy ball." Needless to say, did not cost three hundred. Believe Mom got with soap coupons. Gave to me wrapped in homemade shirt with one long arm hanging down. Then urged me to don long-armed shirt, go out, "show guys." Took photo of me trying to dribble bouncy ball as friend Al held out long arm of shirt, as if to say: Wow, what long arm. In photo, ball bouncing up out of frame. Bottom curve of ball just visible, like moon, Chris M. looking up at ball/moon, amazed/flinching.

However, do not want to break Lilly's heart or harshly remind her of our limitations. God knows she is already often enough harshly reminded of our limitations. For "My Yard" project at school, Leslie Torrini brought in pics of Oriental bridge, plus background info on SGs (place of origin, age, etc.), as did "every other kid in class," whereas Lilly brought in 1940s condom box found last year during aborted attempt to start vegetable garden. Perhaps was bad call re. letting her bring condom box? I thought, being historical, would be good, plus perhaps many would not notice it was condom box. But teacher noticed, pointed out, kids had big hoot, teacher used opportunity to discuss Safe Sex, which was good for class but maybe not so good for Lilly.

As for party, Lilly said she would rather not have one. I

asked why not, sweetie? She said oh no reason. I said is it because of our yard, our house? Is it because you are afraid that, given our small house and bare yard, party might be boring or embarrassing?

At which she burst into tears and said, Oh Daddy.

Actually, one figurine might not be excessive. Or rather, might be excess worth indulging in, due to sad look on her face when she came in on "My Yard" day and dropped condom box on table with sigh.

Maybe "Girl Reading to Little Sister," as that is cheapest? Although maybe giving cheapest sends bad signal? Signals frugality even in midst of attempt to be generous? Maybe best to go big. Go for "Resting Fierceness"?

Put cheetah on Visa, hope she is happily surprised?

(Sept. 14)

Observed Mel Redden today. He did fine. I did fine. He committed minor errors, I caught them all. He made one Recycling error: threw Tab can in wrong bucket. When throwing Tab in wrong bucket, made Ergonomic error, by throwing from far away, missing, having to get up and rethrow. Then made second Ergonomic error: did not squat when picking up Tab to rethrow, but bent at waist, thereby increasing risk of back injury. Mel signed off on my Observations, then asked me to re-Observe. Very smart. Then made no errors. Threw no cans in bucket. Made no Ergonomic errors but just sat very still at desk. So was able to append that to his Record. Parted friends, etc., etc.

One week until L's birthday.

Note to self: Order cheetah.

However, not that simple. Some recent problems with Visa. Full. Past full. Found out at YourItalianKitchen, when Visa refused. Left Pam and kids there, walked rapidly out with big fake smile, drove to ATM. Then scary moment as ATM declined. Nearby wino said ATM broken, directed me to different ATM. Thanked wino with friendly wave as I drove past. Wino gave me finger. Second ATM, thank God, not broken, did not decline.

Arrived winded back at YourItalianKitchen to find Pam on third cup of coffee and kids falling off chairs and tapping aquarium with dimes, waitstaff looking peeved. Paid cash, w/ big apologetic tip. Considered collecting dimes from kids (!). Still, overall nice night. Really fun. Kids showed good manners, until aquarium bit. But problem remains: Visa full. Also AmEx full and Discover nearly full. Called Discover: $200 avail. If we transfer $200 from checking (once paycheck comes in), would then have $400 avail. on Discover, could get cheetah. Although timing problematic. Currently, checking at zero. Paycheck must come, must put paycheck in checking pronto, hope paycheck clears quickly. And then, when doing bills, pick bills totaling $200 to not pay. To defer paying.

Stretched a bit thin these days.

Note to future generations: In our time, are such things as

credit cards. Company loans money, you pay back at high interest rate. Is nice for when you do not actually have money to do thing you want to do (for example, buy extravagant cheetah). You may say, safe in your future time: Wouldn't it be better to simply not do thing you can't afford to do? Easy for you to say! You are not here, in our world, with kids, kids you love, while other people are doing good things for their kids, such as a Heritage Journey to Nice if you are the Mancinis or three weeks wreck-diving off the Bahamas if you are Gary Gold and his tan sleek son Byron.

Limitations so frustrating.

There is so much I want to do and experience and give to kids. Time going by so quickly, kids growing up so fast. If not now, when? When will we give them largesse and sense of generosity? Never been to Hawaii or parasailed or eaten lunch at cafe by ocean, wearing floppy straw hats just purchased on whim. So I worry: Growing up in paucity, won't they become too cautious? Not that they are growing up in paucity. Still, there are things we want but cannot have. If kids raised too cautious, due to paucity, will not world chew them up and spit out? Would like to buy large box, decorate like buried treasure, bury, make map, hide map, lead them to map without appearing to. Then, when they bring map, say: Ridiculous, don't be big dreamers, be cautious, be frugal, world is cruel. And when they persist, and actually find treasure, won't that be an excellent lesson in sticking to it? But how to do? Where to get such a box? What to put in box that doesn't cost too much? How to dig such a big hole, and when?

Always busy on weekends. If had more money, could hire maid, hire garden guy, freeing me up to find box, fill box, bury box. Or have garden guy bury box, after I fill. Or have maid fill. But do not have money for garden guy or maid, or money for treasure box, or treasure to put in it, and in fact do not even have money to buy kit to make map appear ancient.

Still, must fight good fight! Think of Dad. When Mom left Dad, Dad kept going to job. When laid off from job, got paper route. When laid off paper route, got lesser paper route. In time, got better route back. By time Dad died, had job almost as good as original job he had lost. And had paid off most debt incurred after demotion to lesser route.

Note to self: Visit Dad's grave. Bring flowers. Have talk with Dad re. certain things said by me at time of paper routes, due to, could not afford rental tux for prom, but had to wear Dad's old tux, which did not fit. Still, no need to be rude. Was not Dad's fault he was good foot taller than me and therefore pantlegs dragged, hiding Dad's borrowed shoes, which pinched because Dad, though tall, had tiny feet.

Dad good guy. Always worked hard for us and never left us and always brought home candy, even back in sad early days of lesser route.

(Sept. 15)

Damn it. Plan will not work. Cannot get check to Discover on time. Needs time to clear.

So no cheetah.

Must think of something else to get Lilly so we can give to her at small family-only party in kitchen. Or may have to do what Mom sometimes did, which was, when thing not available, wrap picture of thing, with note promising thing. However, note to self: Do not do other thing Mom did, which was, when child tries to redeem, roll eyes, act exasperated, ask child if child thinks money grows on trees.

No. When Lilly comes to me with coupon, surprise with generosity by taking her to glamorous lunch at best place in town, all dressed up, owner comes over and says, w/French accent, *Oh I see it is someone's special day,* and Lilly blushes (note to self: Learn French phrase meaning *Yes, yes, it is her birthday*), after which we go shopping for figurines, and to surprise her, I buy her not just one, but two figurines, and better, more expensive ones than cheap crap in catalog.

Note to self: Find ad with pic of cheetah, for IOU coupon. Was on little desk but have not seen. Possibly used to record phone message on? Possibly used to pick up little thing cat spit out?

Note to self: Find out what is best restaurant in town.

Poor Lilly. Her sweet hopeful face when tiny, wearing Burger King crown, and now this? She did not know was destined to be, not princess, but poor girl. Poorish girl. Girl not-the-richest.

No party, no present. Possibly no pic of cheetah in IOU. Could draw cheetah but might then think she was getting camel. Or not getting camel, rather. Am not best drawer. Ha ha! Must keep spirits up. Laughter best medicine etc., etc.

Someday, I'm sure, dreams will come true. But when? Why not now? Why not?

Have had such a headache for three straight days.

(Sept. 20)

Sorry for silence but wow!

Was too happy/busy to write!

Friday most incredible day ever! Do not need to even write down, as will never forget this awesome day! But will record for future generations. Nice for them to know good luck and happiness real and possible! In America of my time, want them to know, anything possible!

Weird to look at previous entry and see phrase "Why not now?" because *exactly*! That is exactly what happened!

Wow wow wow is all I can say! Remember how, above, always buy lunchtime Scratch-Off ticket? Have I said? Maybe did not say? Well, Friday, won TEN GRAND!! Every Friday, to reward self for good week, stop at store near home, treat self to Butterfinger, plus Scratch-Off ticket. Sometimes, if hard week, two Butterfingers. Sometimes, if very hard week, three Butterfingers. But if three Butterfingers, no Scratch-Off. But Friday won TEN GRAND!! On Scratch-Off! Dropped both Butterfingers, stood there holding dime used to Scratch, mouth hanging open. Kind of reeled into magazine rack. Guy took ticket, read ticket, said: Winner! Guy came out, righted magazine rack, shook my hand.

Then said we would get check, check for TEN GRAND, within week.

Raced home on foot, forgetting car. Raced back for car. Halfway back, thought what the heck, raced home on foot. Pam raced out, said where is car? Showed her Scratch-Off ticket, she stood stunned in yard.

Are we rich now? Thomas said, racing out, dragging Ferber by collar.

Not rich, Pam said.

Richer, I said.

Richer, Pam said. Damn.

Then we all danced around yard, Ferber looking witless at sudden dancing, then doing dance of own, by chasing own tail.

Then of course had to decide how to use. That night in bed Pam said partially pay off credit cards? My feeling was yes, o.k., could. But did not seem to me exciting and also did not seem all that exciting to her.

Pam: It would be nice to do something special for Lilly's birthday.

Me: Me too, exactly, yes!

Pam: She could use something, she has really been down.

Me: You know what, let's do it.

Because Lilly our oldest, we have soft spot for her, soft spot that is also like worry spot.

So we hatched up scheme, then did.

Which was: went to Greenway Landscaping, had them do total new yard design, incl. ten rose bushes + cedar pathway

+ pond + small hot-tub + four-SG arrangement! Big fun part was, how soon could it be done? Plus could it be done secret? Greenway said, for price, could do in one day, while kids at school. (Note to self: write letter praising Melanie, Greenway gal: super facilitator.)

Step two was, send out secret invites to surprise party to be held on evening of day of yard completion, i.e., tomorrow, i.e., that is why so silent in terms of this book for last week, sorry, sorry, have just been superbusy!

Pam and I worked so well together, like in old days, so nice and close, total agreement, that night when arrangements all made, went to bed early (!!). (Masseuse scenario, do not ask!)

Sorry if corny.

Am just happy.

Sometimes so busy do not see her/she does not see me. But when we do see each other, is like early days, for example first date at Melody Lake when, entering Spelunker's Cave, we kissed near crowd of grey-beard animatrons, in smell of chlorine mist from nearby bright-blue waterfall.

Was beginning of our beautiful story.

Am so happy.

Note to future generations: Happiness possible. And when happy, so much better than opposite, i.e., sad. Hopefully you know! I knew, but forgot. Got used to being slightly sad! Slightly sad, due to stress, due to worry vis-a-vis limitations. But now, wow, no: happy!

Tomorrow big party for Lilly.

———

(September 21! Lilly B-Day(!))

There are days so perfect you feel: This is what life about. When old, will feel whole life worth it, because I got to experience this perfect day.

Today that kind of day.

Maybe too excited to tell in order, plus tired after long great day. But will try.

In morning kids go off to school per usual. Greenway comes at ten. Nice guys. Big guys! One w/Mohawk. Yard done by two (!). Roses in, fountain in, pathway in. SG truck arrives at three. SGs exit truck, stand shyly near fence while rack installed. Rack nice. Opted for "Lexington" (mid-range in terms of price): bronze uprights w/Colonial caps, Ezy-Releese levers.

SGs already in white smocks. Microline already strung through. SGs holding microline slack in hands, like mountain climbers holding rope. Only no mountain (!). One squatting, others standing polite/nervous, one sniffing new roses. She gives timid wave, other says something to her, like saying: Hey, not supposed to wave. But I wave back, like saying: In this household, is o.k. to wave.

Doctor monitors installation by law. So young! Looks like should be working at Wendy's. Says we can watch hoist or not. Gives me meaningful look, cuts eyes at Pam, as in: wife squeamish? Pam somewhat squeamish. Sometimes does not like to handle raw chicken. I say let's go inside, put candles on cake.

Soon, knock on door: doctor says hoist all done.

Me: So can we have a look?

Him: Totally.

We step out. SGs up now, approx. three feet off ground, smiling, swaying in slight breeze. Order, left to right: Tami (Laos), Gwen (Moldova), Lisa (Somalia), Betty (Philippines). Effect amazing. Having so often seen similar configuration in yards of others more affluent, makes own yard seem suddenly affluent, you feel different about self, as if at last you are in step with peers and time in which living.

Pond great. Roses great. Path, hot tub great.

Everything set.

Could not believe we had pulled this off.

Picked Lilly up early at school. Lilly all hangdog because her b-day and no one said Happy B-Day at breakfast, and no party and no gifts so far, plus now has to go to doctor, for shot?

Because that was ruse.

In car, pretended to be lost. Lilly (discouraged): Daddy, how can you be lost when Hunneke our doctor forever? (Pam worked this out in advance with nurse, who, when I finally "found" office, came out, said the doctor was sick, too sick to give shot: the first of series of super surprises for Lilly!)

Meanwhile, at home: Pam, Thomas, Eva scramble to decorate. Food delivered (BBQ from Snakey's). Friends arrive. So when Lilly gets out of car, what does she see but whole new yard full of all friends from school sitting at new picnic table near new hot tub (note to self: write note praising kids for admirable restraint/keeping secret), and new line of four SGs, and Lilly literally bursts into tears of happiness!

Then more tears as shiny pink packages unwrapped, "Resting Fierceness" plus "Girl Reading to Little Sister" revealed. Lilly touched I had remembered exact figurines. Plus "Summer Daze" (hobo-clown fishing ($380)), which she hadn't even requested (just to prove largesse). Several more waves of happy tears, hugs, right in front of friends, as if gratitude/affection for us greater than fear of rebuke from friends.

Party guests played usual games, "Crack the Whip," etc., etc. Somehow, playing in beautiful new yard energized games. Kids joyful, thanked us for inviting, several said they loved yard. Several parents lingered after, saying they loved yard.

And my God the look on Lilly's face as all left!

Know she will always remember today.

Only one slight negative: after party, during cleanup, Eva stomps away, picks up cat too roughly the way she sometimes does when mad. Cat scratches her, runs over to Ferber, claws Ferber. Ferber dashes away, stumbles into table, roses bought for Lilly crash down, on Ferber.

We find Eva in closet.

Pam: Sweetie, sweetie, what is it?

Eva: I don't like it. It's not nice.

Thomas (rushing over with cat to show he is master of cat): They want to, Eva. They like applied for it.

Pam: Don't say "like."

Thomas: They applied for it.

Pam: Where they're from, the opportunities are not so good.

Me: It helps them take care of the people they love.

Eva facing wall, lower lip out in her pre-crying way.

Then I get idea: Go to kitchen, page through Personal Statements. Yikes. Worse than I thought: Laotian (Tami) applied due to two sisters already in brothels. Moldovan (Gwen) has cousin who thought was becoming window washer in Germany, but no: sex slave in Kuwait (!). Somali (Lisa) watched father + little sister die of AIDs, same tiny thatch hut, same year. Filipina (Betty) has little brother "very skilled for computer," parents cannot afford high school, have lived in tiny lean-to with three other families since their own tiny lean-to slid down hillside in earthquake.

I opt for "Betty," go back to closet, read "Betty" aloud.

Me: Does that help? Do you understand now? Can you kind of imagine her little brother, in a good school, because of her, because of us?

Eva: If we want to help them, why can't we just give them the money?

Me: Oh, sweetie.

Pam: Let's go look. Let's see do they look sad.

(Do not look sad. Are in fact quietly chatting in moonlight.)

At window, Eva quiet. Deep well. So sensitive. Even when tiny, Eva sensitive. When former cat Squiggy dying, Eva slept beside cat bed, gave Squiggy water via eyedropper. Kind heart. But I worry, Pam worries: if kid too sensitive, kid goes out in world, world rips kid's guts out, i.e., some toughness req'd?

Lilly, on other hand, wrote all thank-you notes tonight in one sitting, mopped kitchen without being asked, then was out in yard w/flashlight, picking up Ferber area with new poop-scoop she apparently had ridden down on bike to buy w/own money at FasMart (!).

(Sep. 22)

Happy period continues.

Everyone at work curious re. Scratch-Off win. Brought pics of yard into work, posted in cubicle, folks came by, admired. Steve Z. asked could he drop by house sometime, see yard in person. This a first: Steve Z. has never previously given me time of day. Even asked my advice: where did I buy winning Scratch-Off, how many Scratch-Offs do I typically buy, Greenway = reputable company?

Embarrassed to admit how happy this made me.

At lunch, went to mall, bought four new shirts. Running joke in department vis-à-vis: I only have two shirts. Not so. But have three similar blue shirts and two identical yellow shirts. Hence confusion. Do not generally buy new clothes for self. Have always felt it more important for kids to have new clothes, i.e., did not want other kids saying my kids have only two shirts etc., etc. As for Pam, Pam very beautiful, raised w/money. Do not want former wealthy beauty wearing same clothes over and over, feeling: when I was young, had so many clothes, but now, due to him (i.e., me), no, badly dressed.

Correction: Pam not raised wealthy. Pam's father = farmer in small town. Had biggest farm on edge of small town. So, relative to girls on smaller, poorer farms, Pam = rich girl. If same farm near bigger town, farm only average, but no. town so small, modest farm = potato.

Anyway, Pam deserves best.

On way home, stopped at store where had bought winning Scratch-Off. Bought Scratch-Off, plus four Butterfingers. Thought of bad old days, when, in laughable old shirt, would feel bad/guilty for buying even one Butterfinger.

Guy behind counter remembered me, said: Hey, Mr. Scratch-Off, Mr. Big Winner!

Everyone in store looked. I waved Butterfingers, two per hand, like scepters, mini-scepters, went out feeling happy.

Why happy?

Nice to win, be winner, be known as winner.

Came home, took detour around side of house to peek at yard. Yard amazing: fish hovering near lily pads, bees buzzing around roses, SGs in fresh white smocks, shaft of sun falling across lawn, dust motes rising up w/sleepy late summer feeling, LifeStyleServices team (i.e., Greenway folks who come by 3x/day to give SGs meals/water, take SGs to

SmallJon in back of van, deal with feminine issues, etc, etc.) hard at work in yard.

Greenway gal: Kind of magic back here.

Inside, found Leslie Torrini over (!). This = huge. Leslie never over solo before. Says she likes the way our SGs hang close to pond, are thus reflected in pond. Calls home, demands pond. Leslie's mother calls Leslie spoiled brat, says no pond. This = big score for Lilly. Not that we are glad when someone else not glad. But Leslie so often glad when Lilly not glad, maybe is o.k. if, just once, Leslie = little bit sad, while Lilly = riding high?

Girls go into yard, stay in yard for long time. Pam and I peek out. Girls getting along? Girls have heads together in shade of trees, exchanging girlish intimacies, cementing Lilly's status as pal of Leslie? Can't tell. Girls facing away.

Leslie's mother arrives (in BMW). Leslie, Leslie's mother bicker briefly re. pond.

Leslie's mom: Les, love, you already have three streams.

Leslie (caustic): Is a stream a pond, Maman?

Leslie and mom leave.

Lilly gives me grateful peck on cheek, runs upstairs singing happy tune.

Am so happy. Feel so lucky. What did we do to deserve? In part, yes: luck. Scratch-Off win = luck. But as saying goes, luck = ninety percent skill. Or preparation? Preparation = ninety percent skill? Skill = ninety percent luck? Cannot exactly remember saying. Anyway, to our credit, managed our good luck well. Did not go nuts, buy boat, buy drugs (!), fly off handle, become discontent, seek lovers, get cocky. Just took good hard look at family, discerned what family member (Lilly) needed, quietly/humbly made sure she got.

Note to self: Try to extend positive feelings associated with Scratch-Off win into all areas of life. Be bigger presence at work. Race up ladder (joyfully, w/smile on face), get raise. Get in best shape of life, start dressing nicer. Learn guitar? Make point of noticing beauty of world? Why not educate self re. birds, flowers, trees, constellations, become true citizen of natural world, walk around neighborhood w/kids, patiently teaching kids names of birds, flowers, etc. etc.? Why not take kids to Europe? Kids have never been. Have never, in Alps, had hot chocolate in mountain café, served by kindly white-haired innkeeper, who finds them so sophisticated/ friendly relative to usual snotty/rich American kids (who always ignore his pretty but crippled daughter w/braids) that he shows them secret hiking path to incredible glade, kids frolic in glade, sit with crippled pretty girl on grass, later say it was most beautiful day of their lives, keep in touch with crippled girl via email, we arrange surgery here for her, surgeon so touched he agrees to do surgery for free, she is on front page of our paper, we are on front page of their paper in Alps?

Ha ha.

Just happy.

Hence these fantastical speculations.

(Actually have never been to Europe myself. Dad felt portions there too small. Then Dad lost job, got paper route, portion size = moot point.)

Have been sleepwalking through life, future reader. Can see that now. Scratch-Off win was like wake-up call. In rush to graduate college, win Pam, get job, make babies, move ahead in job, forgot former feeling of special destiny I used to have when tiny, sitting in cedar-smelling bedroom closet, looking up at blowing trees through high windows, feeling I would someday do something great.

Hereby resolve to live life in new and more powerful way, starting THIS MOMENT (!)

(Sept. 23)

Eva being a pain.

As I may have mentioned above, Eva = sensitive. This good, Pam and I feel: this = sign of intelligence. But Eva seems to have somehow gotten idea that sensitivity = effective way to get attention, i.e., has developed tendency to set herself apart from others, possibly as way of distinguishing self, i.e., casting self as better, more refined than others? Has, in past, refused to eat meat, sit on leather seats, use plastic forks made in China. Is endearing enough when little kid does. But Eva getting older now, this tendency to object on principle starting to feel a bit precious + becoming fundamental to how she views self?

Family life of our time sometimes seems like game of Whac-a-Mole, future reader. Future generations still have?

Plastic mole emerges, you whack with hammer, he dies, falls, another emerges, you whack, kill? Perhaps may seem like strange/violent game to you, future reader? Who no longer even need to eat to live? Just levitate all day, smiling warmly at one another? Sometimes seems that, as soon as one kid happy, another kid "pops up," i.e., registers complaint, requiring parent to "whack" kid, i.e., address complaint.

Apparently now Eva's turn.

Today Eva's teacher, Ms. Ross, sent home note: Eva acting out. Eva grouchy, Eva stamped foot, Eva threw fish food container at John M. when John M. asked for his turn to feed fish. This not like Eva, Ms. R. says: Eva sweetest, kindest kid in class.

Also, Eva's artwork has recently gone odd.

Sample odd artwork enclosed:

Typical house. (Can tell is meant to be our house by mock cherry tree = swirl of pink.) In yard, SGs frowning. One ("Betty") having thought in cartoon balloon: OUCH! THIS SURE HERTS. Second ("Gwen") pointing long bony finger at house: THANKS LODES. Third ("Lisa"), tears rolling down cheeks: WHAT IF I AM YOUR DAUHTER?

Pam: Well. This doesn't seem to be going away.

Me: No, it does not.

Took Eva for drive. Drove through Eastridge, Lemon Hills. Pointed out houses w/SGs. Had Eva keep count. In end, of approx 50 houses, 39 had.

Eva: So just because everyone is doing it, that makes it right.

This cute. Eva parroting me, Pam.

On Waddle Duck Crossing, eight-SG arrangement: SGs holding hands, nice (paper-doll) effect. All seem to be singing together. Three toddlers racing around rack, two puppies chasing toddlers.

Me: Wow. That looks pretty miserable.

(Eva sharp, Eva witty. Hence will often joke w/Eva.)

Eva silent.

Stopped at Fritz's Chillhouse, had banana split, Eva had SnowMelt, we sat on big wooden crocodile, watched sun go down.

Eva: I don't even—I don't even get it how they're not dead.

Suddenly occurred to me, w/little gust of relief: Eva resisting in part because she does not understand basic science of thing. Asked Eva if she even knew what Semplica Pathway was. Did not. Drew human head on napkin, explained: Lawrence Semplica = doctor + smart cookie. Found way to route microline through brain that does no damage, causes no pain. Technique uses lasers to make pilot route. Microline then threaded through w/silk leader. Microline goes in here (touched Eva's temple), comes out here (touched other). Is very gentle, does not hurt, SGs out during whole deal.

Then decided to level w/Eva.

Explained: Lilly at critical juncture. Next year, Lilly will start high school. Mommy and Daddy want Lilly to enter high school able to hold her head up, as confident young woman, feeling her family as good/affluent as any other family, her yard approx. in ballpark of yards of peers, i.e., not so far out of whack as previously, i.e., not overt source of embarrassment for Lilly.

This too much to ask?

Eva quiet.

Could see wheels turning.

Eva wild about Lilly, would walk in front of train for Lilly.

Then shared story w/Eva re. summer job I had in high school, at Señor Tasty's (taco place). Was hot, was greasy, boss mean, boss always goosing us with tongs. By time I went home, hair always completely greasy + shirt stunk of grease. No way I could do that job now. But then? Actually enjoyed: flirted with counter girls, participated in pranks with other employees (hid tongs of mean boss, slipped magazine down own pants so that, when mean boss tong-goosed me, did not hurt, mean boss = baffled).

Point is, I said, everything relative. SGs have lived very different lives from us. Their lives brutal, harsh, unpromising. What looks scary/unpleasant to us may not be so scary/unpleasant to them, i.e., they have seen worse.

Eva: You flirted with girls?

Me: I did. Don't tell Mom.

That got little smile.

Believe I somewhat broke through with Eva. Hope so. At any rate, am glad I tried. When Mom and Dad divorcing, Dad took me for milkshake, broke news re. divorce. Was always grateful to Dad for this. Felt good to know he was thinking of me even in what must have been sad + dark time for him.

Mom was having affair with Ted DeWitt, guy from work. DeWitt always flattering Mom, saying she looked pretty, saying she was only reason he even got up in morning. Mom not used to this. Dad loved Mom. But Dad laconic. Dad not one to blab about his love. Dad loved in quiet, steady way. For their tenth anniversary, Dad bought Mom power sander (!). Dad's pet name for Mom = Stretch. (Mom tall.) Dad used to joke that Mom looked like tall boy. Would sometimes walk into kitchen, pretend to be startled by presence of tall boy at sink. Mom, charmed by DeWitt, began sneaking away to hotel with DeWitt, fell in love with DeWitt. (Did not know any of this at time. Only found out years later, when Dad, at end of life, told me all.)

When Sister Dolores caught wind of divorce, Sister kept class in from recess, gave class big speech vis-à-vis divorce = mortal sin, afterlife no picnic for divorced people, forced whole class to pray for souls of Mom and Dad. Everyone glaring at me, as in: because of you, we get no recess.

Whole thing painful.

Is still painful.

Hence my focus on being good father/husband, providing stable platform for kids.

Discussed Eva situation w/ Pam tonight. Pam, as usual, offered sound counsel: Go slow, be patient, Eva bright, Eva savvy. In another month, Eva will have adjusted, forgotten all about, will once again be usual happy self.

Love Pam.

Pam my rock.

(Sept 30)

Sorry for silence.

Crazy thing happened this week.

Monday, Todd Grassberger died (!).

Future readers know Todd? Have I mentioned? Probably have not mentioned. Todd not close friend. Just work colleague. Todd and I had running joke re. I had never returned fire-wire I had borrowed. In fact, was company fire-wire, not his. He knew. I knew he knew. Was just our joke.

Day started out fine. Beautiful Indian summer day. Fire drill in morning. Whole complex emptied into outdoor courtyard. Day so beautiful, no one minded. Everyone lounging on berms, urging caution. Fun to see people of different companies. Like seeing members of different tribes. NabroMax = nerds, calculating temperature needed to destroy, by fire, entire complex. Oorjd = design firm. Has many hippies, prettiest girls. Many Oorjd folks lying on backs on berms, looking up at clouds. One guy playing small wood flute.

When all-clear sounded, everyone booed, all filed sadly back inside.

Then, at two, word rippled through office: Todd dead. Had heart attack at dry cleaner (!), just now, during lunch.

All afternoon, no one working. Everyone stunned, milling around, trying to process fact that Todd = dead. Under Todd's desk: pair of hiking boots. Against one wall: walking stick Todd used to take on lunchtime walks in woods.

Weird sunshower around three.

Linda Hertney: It's like a final goodbye from Todd. (Linda = nut. Once claimed crow on ledge was reincarnation of her dead husband. Said she could tell by way crow's head was cocked disapprovingly at large lunch she was eating.)

Then storm over, parking lot glistening.

All evening found myself looking afresh at Pam, kids. Everything suddenly precious. Said prayer before dinner. Do not usually pray before dinner. But tonight, held hands, prayed. Prayed we would be grateful for our good fortune, grateful for each other. Prayed we would remember that various ups/downs we may experience as family = small bumps in road compared with this.

Prayed for Todd, prayed for Todd's family.

Just nights ago Todd was in own house, doing whatever Todd did at night: taking change out of pockets, having laugh with kids, petting dog, thinking of future, tossing dirty clothes in hamper.

Where is Todd tonight (?!).

(Oct. 1)

Todd Grassberger funeral today at Ukrainian church downtown.

Todd apparently from humble roots.

Priest = long-haired guy in cassock. Sings/chants whole service, in Ukrainian, from memory. As he chants/paces, cassock rope swings. Scary guy. Very intense. Sermon: Why this surprising? Did you think you were going to live forever? Only difference between you, sitting there anticipating rest of your day, and Todd, in coffin, bound for eternal home in cold earth? Is heartbeat. Feel that, people? In your chests? That is thin line between you and grave. So why do you live like you are eternal? That foolish, you are fools. This scary? This not scary! This truth, this reality!

Shouts: Shall we wake up? Shall we?

Everyone staring big-eyed at priest. Except usual congregants, who seem to have heard all before.

Priest goes on: Which of us will die tonight? Do we think he is being facetious? That shows we are dopes. Any one of us could die tonight, die right now, suddenly come up short of breath, keel over in pew, be with Todd in earth in wink of eye.

Suddenly, from downstairs kitchen: smell of roast beef. Happy chatter from church ladies down in kitchen. Smell of roast beef + sound of pots clanking, plates being set out = appealing.

People shifting in pews due to amazing smell of beef.

Todd's two brothers come to lectern, make tributes.

Older brother: Todd sweet, Todd funny, Todd a powerful force in his life. Will never forget wonder that was Todd. Younger brother: Yes, Todd superstrong person, Todd = bull. Although Todd could be somewhat firm, Todd did younger brother much good, in long run, by teaching him how to stand up for self. That is to say, having been pushed around by Todd throughout entire childhood, nothing can now faze younger brother, i.e., no bully in outside world will ever be equal of Todd. But Todd so great, Todd the best. Todd so smart, so good-looking, no wonder Todd's mom + dad always treated him (younger brother) like afterthought. But Todd so caring, so perceptive, Todd understood this, would sometimes console younger brother by saying that he (younger brother) was perfectly fine in own way, often just before breaking pact they had made re. Wednesday night being younger brother's night to borrow Dad's car, thereby ruining younger brother's chance to see girl he really liked, possible love of life, girl he eventually lost to dope from Selden, dope whose own older brother apparently more inclined than Todd to give his younger brother decent shot at family car.

Todd's younger brother, breathless, pauses at lectern. Can't seem to stop self.

Plunges ahead.

But Todd great, Todd so great, Todd will surely be missed. Todd taught everyone in family important lesson: although person might be strong, bellicose, ambitious, slightly blind to needs of others, still, that does not mean person not greatest, most amazing brother ever who, occasionally, as if to spite self, might suddenly, surprising all, do some reasonably thoughtful thing.

Younger brother, seemingly perplexed by own tribute, then led away from lectern by scowling older brother hissing something in undertone.

Todd's widow approaches lectern. Can't seem to speak. Three little girls clinging to her skirt. Widow hands microphone to smallest girl.

Smallest girl: Bye, Daddy.

Lunch good. Lunch beyond good. Funeral so sad, lunch = heaven. Eat three roast beef sandwiches in row off paper plate. Outside, yellow tree blowing in wind. Single yellow leaf blows in through open basement window. Watch it come down, land near my shoe.

Think: Life beautiful.

So glad am not dead.

If/when I die, do not want Pam lonely. Want her to remarry, have full life. As long as new husband is nice guy. Gentle guy. Religious guy. Very caring + good to kids. But kids not fooled. Kids prefer dead dad (i.e., me) to religious guy. Pale, boring, religious guy, with no oomph, who wears weird sweaters and is always a little sad, due to, cannot get boner, due to physical ailment.

Ha ha.

Death very much on my mind tonight, future reader. Can it be true? That I will die? That Pam, kids will die? Is awful. Why were we put here, so inclined to love, when end of our story = death? That harsh. That cruel. Do not like.

Note to self: try harder, in all things, to be better person.

At home, gathered kids around. Asked kids to join me in new resolution. Told kids life short, we must make every moment count, live each day as if it were our last. If they have dream, they must do. If they have urge to try thing, must try. Will they promise? If I have made one mistake in life, it is that I have been too passive. Do not want them making same mistake. Must dare, strive, be brave. What is worst that could happen? They will be known as innovator, hero, prophet (!). Was Paul Revere timid, Edison cautious, Jesus superpolite? At end of life, they will not regret what they have done, will only regret what they failed to do.

Then bedtime. Bedtime sometimes rough: Pam, tired from long day with kids, will sometimes get harsh with kids at slightest resistance. Kids, tired from school, will sometimes get lippy with Pam at first sign of Pam getting harsh. Sometimes nighty-night = kids at top of stairs screaming down, Pam at bottom of stairs screaming up. Sometimes book or shoe will come whizzing downstairs past Pam.

Tonight, however, bedtime easy. Kids, feeling truth of my words re. death, file upstairs quietly. Thomas runs back down to give me hug, Eva shoots me long (admiring?) look from landing.

Such dear kids.

One of pleasures of parenting, future reader: parent can positively influence kid, make moment kid will remember for rest of life, moment that alters his/her trajectory, opens up his/her heart + mind.

(Oct. 2)
    Shit.
    Fuck.

Family hit by absolute thunderclap, future reader.

Will explain.

This morning, Thomas and Lilly sitting sleepily at table, Eva still in bed, Pam making eggs, Ferber under her feet, hoping scrap of food will drop. Thomas, eating bagel, drifts to window.

Thomas: Wow. What the heck. Dad? You better get over here.

Go to window.

SGs gone.

Totally gone (!).

Race out. Rack empty. Microline gone. Gate open. Take somewhat frantic run up block, to see if is any sign of them. Is not.

Race back inside. Call Greenway, call police. Cops arrive, scour yard. Cop shows me microline drag mark in mud near gate. Says this actually good news: with microline still in, will be easier to locate SGs, as microline limits how fast they can walk, since, fleeing in group, joined at head by microline, they are thereby forced to take babysteps, so one does not get too far behind/ahead of others, hence causing yank on microline, yank that could damage brain of one yanked.

Other cop says yes, that would be case if SGs on foot. But come on, he says, SGs not on foot, SGs off in activist van somewhere, laughing butts off.

Me: Activists.

First cop: Yeah, you know: Women4Women, Citizens for Economic Parity, Semplica Rots in Hell.

Second cop: Fourth incident this month.

First cop: Those gals didn't get down by themselves.

Me: Why would they do that? They chose to be here. Why would they go off with some total—

Cops laugh.

First cop: Smelling that American dream, baby.

Kids beyond freaked. Kids huddled near fence.

School bus comes and goes.

Greenway field rep (Rob) arrives. Rob = tall, thin, bent. Looks like archery bow, if archery bow had pierced ear + long hair like pirate, was wearing short leather vest.

Rob immediately drops bombshell: says he is sorry to have to be more or less a hardass in our time of trial, but is legally obligated to inform us that, per our agreement w/ Greenway, if SGs not located within three weeks, we will, at that time, become responsible for full payment of the required Replacement Debit.

Pam: Wait, the what?

Per Rob, Replacement Debit = $100/month, per individual, per each month still remaining on their Greenway contract at time of loss (!). Betty (21 months remaining) = $2100; Tami (13 months) = $1300; Gwen (18 months) = $1800; Lisa (34 months (!)) = $3400.

Total = $2100 + $1300 + $1800 + $3400 = $8600.

Pam: Fucksake.

Rob: Believe me, I know, that's a lot of money, I'm primarily a songwriter, right? But our take on it is—or, you know, their take on it, Greenway's take, is that we—or they—made an initial investment, and, I mean, obviously, that was not cheap, just in terms of like visas and airfares and all?

Pam: No one said anything to us about this.

Me: At all.

Rob: Huh. Who was on your account again?

Me: Melanie?

Rob: Right, yeah, I had a feeling. With Melanie, Melanie was sometimes rushing through things to close the deal. Especially with Package A folks, who were going chintzy in the first place? No offense. Anyway, which is why she's gone. If you want to yell at her, go to Home Depot, she's second in charge of Paint, probably lying her butt off about which color is which.

Feel angry, violated: someone came into our yard in dark of night, while kids sleeping nearby, stole? Stole from us? Stole $8600, plus initial cost of SGs (approx. $7400)?

Pam (to cop): How often do you find them?

First cop: Who?

Pam glares at cop. (Pam = fierce when defending family.)

Second cop: Honestly? I'd have to say rarely.

First cop: More like never.

Second cop: Well, never yet.

First cop: Right. There's always a first time.

Cops leave.

Pam (to Rob): So what happens if we don't pay?

Me: Can't pay.

Rob uncomfortable, Rob blushing.

Rob: Well, that would be more of an issue for Legal.

Pam: You'd sue us?

Rob: I wouldn't. They would. I mean, that's what they do. They—what's that word? They garner your—

Pam (harshly): Garnish.

Rob: Sorry. Sorry about all this. Melanie, wow, I am going to snap your head back using that stupid braid of yours. Just kidding, I never even talk to her. But the thing is: all this is in your contract. You guys read your contract, right?

Silence.

Me: Well, we were kind of in a hurry. We were throwing a party.

Rob: Oh sure, I remember that party. That was some party. We were all discussing that.

Rob leaves.

Pam livid.

Pam: You know what? Fuck 'em. Let 'em sue. I'm not paying. That's obscene. They can have the stupid house.

Lilly: Are we losing the house?

Me: We're not losing the—

Pam: You don't think? What do you think happens if you owe someone nine grand and can't pay? I think we lose the house.

Me: Look, let's calm down, no need to get all—

Eva's lower lip out in pre-crying way. Think: oh great, nice parenting, arguing + swearing + raising specter of loss of house in front of tightly wound kid already upset by troubling events of day.

Then Eva bursts into tears, starts mumbling sorry sorry sorry.

Pam: Oh sweetie, I was just being silly, we're not going to lose the house. Mommy and Daddy would never let that—

Light goes on in my head.

Me: Eva. You didn't.

Look in Eva's eyes says: I did.

Pam: Did what?

Thomas: Eva did it?

Lilly: How could Eva do it? She's only eight. I couldn't even—

Eva leads us outside, shows us how she did: Dragged out stepladder, stood on stepladder at one end of microline, released left-hand EzyReleese lever, microline sagged. Eva then dragged stepladder to other end, released right-hand EzyReleese. At that point, microline completely loose, SGs standing on ground.

SGs briefly confer.

And off they go.

Am so mad. Eva has made huge mess here. Huge mess for us, yes, but also for SGs. Where are SGs now? In good place? Is it good when illegal fugitives in strange land have no money, no food, no water, are forced to hide in woods, swamp, etc., connected via microline like chain gang? As for Thomas and Lilly, they think it is a big joke to trick own parents? I remember how Thomas stepped to window, acted all surprised SGs gone. Thomas = stinker. As for Lilly: We do so much for Lilly's b-day, this is thanks we get?

Am hot under collar. Inadvertently say all of above out loud.

Kids stunned. Kids have never seen me so mad.

Thomas: Daddy, we didn't know!

Lilly: We honestly didn't!

Thomas, pulling at own hair, runs outside. Lilly bursts into tears, stomps out of room, dragging (stunned) Eva by hand.

Eva (crestfallen, to me): But you said, you said that thing, that thing about being brave—

Note to future generations: sometimes, in our time, families get into dark place. Family feels: we are losers, everything we do is wrong. Parents fight at high volume, blaming one another for disastrous situation. Dad kicks wall, puts hole in wall near fridge, family skips lunch. Tension too high for all to sit at same table. This unbearable. This makes person (father) doubt value of whole enterprise, i.e., makes father (me) wonder if humans would not be better off living alone, individually, in woods, minding own beeswax, not loving anyone.

Today like that for us.

Stormed out to garage. Stupid squirrel/mouse stain still there after all these weeks. Decided to take care of stain once and for all. Used bleach + hose to eradicate. In resulting calm, sat on wheelbarrow, had to laugh at situation. Won Scratch-Off, greatest luck of life, quickly converted greatest luck of life into greatest fiasco of life.

Laughter turned to tears.

Felt so bad for harsh things I just now said to kids.

Pam came out, asked had I been crying? I said no, got dust in eyes from cleaning garage. Pam not buying. Pam gave me little side hug + hip nudge, to say: You were crying, is o.k., is difficult time, I know.

Pam: Come on inside. Let's get things back to normal. We'll get through this. The kids are dying in there, they feel so bad.

Went inside.

Kids at kitchen table.

Could see in eyes of kids they were anxious to forgive, be forgiven. Lilly and Thomas did not know. I said I knew they did not know, do not know why I said I thought they knew.

Opened arms, Thomas and Lilly rushed over.

Eva stayed sitting.

When Eva tiny, had big head of black curls. Would stand on couch, eating cereal from coffee mug, dancing to sound in head, flicking around cord from window blinds.

Now this: Eva sitting w/ head in hands, like heartbroken old lady mourning loss of vigorous flower of youth etc., etc.

Went over, scooped Eva up.

Poor thing shaking in my arms.

Eva (whispers): I didn't know we would lose the house.

Me: We're not—we're not going to lose the house. Mommy and I going to figure this out.

Sent kids off to watch TV.

Pam: So. You want me to call Dad?

Did not want Pam calling Pam's dad.

Pam's dad's first name = Rich. Actually calls self "Farmer Rich." Is funny because he is rich farmer. Farmer Rich = very rich + very strict. In terms of me, does not like me. Has said at various times that I 1) am not hard worker and 2) had better watch self in terms of weight and 3) had better watch self in terms of credit cards.

Farmer Rich in very good shape, with no credit cards.

Farmer Rich not fan of SGs. Gave big lecture to all last Christmas: feels having SGs = "show-offy move." Thinks anything fun = "show-offy move." Even going to movie = show-offy move. Going to car wash, i.e., not doing self, in driveway = show-offy move. Once, when visiting, looked dubiously at me when I said I had to get root canal. What, I was thinking, root canal = show-offy move? But no: just disapproved of dentist I had chosen, due to he had seen dentist's TV ad, felt dentist having TV ad = show-offy move.

So did not want Pam calling Farmer Rich.

Tell Pam we must try our best to handle this ourselves.

Got out bills, did mock payment exercise: If we pay mortgage, heat bill, AmEx, plus $200 in bills we deferred last time, would be down near zero ($12.78 remaining). If we defer AmEx + Visa, that would free up $880. If, in addition, we skip mortgage payment, NiMo bill, life insurance premium, that would still only free up measly total of $3100.

Me: Shit.

Pam: Maybe I'll email him. You know. Just see what he says.

Pam upstairs emailing Farmer Rich as I write.

(Oct. 6)

Will skip description of work. Work not important right now. When I got home, Pam standing in doorway w/email from Farmer Rich.

Farmer Rich = bastard.

Will quote in part:

Let us now speak of what you intend to do with the requested money. Will you be putting it aside for a college fund? You will not. Investing in real estate? No. Given a chance to plant some seeds, you flushed those valuable seeds (dollars) away. And for what? A display some find pretty. Well, I do not find it pretty. I see the young people here doing the same. Old people too. And it makes no more sense here than there. Since when are people on display a desirable sight? Others here are do-gooders in our church and cite conditions of poverty. OK, that is fine. But it appears you will soon have a situation of poverty within your own walls. And physician heal thyself is a motto I have oft remembered when tempted to put my oar in relative to some social cause or another. Although am not against dropping off a ham at our abused woman home now and then. So am going to say no. You people have walked your-

selves into some deep water and must now walk yourselves out, teaching your kids (and selves) a valuable lesson from which, in the longterm, you and yours will benefit.

Me: Ouch.

Pam called Farmer Rich, begged Farmer Rich. Farmer Rich laid into her on phone re. money, re. our entire history of money, i.e., our entire approach to life = wasteful. Farmer Rich said do not ask again. We have dropped in his estimation via initial jackass move + subsequent desperate show of hubris in attempt to rectify initial jackass move in boneheaded manner.

So that = that.

Long silence.

Pam: Jesus. Isn't this just like us?

Do not know what she means. Or, rather, know, but do not agree. Or, rather, agree, but wish she would not say. Why say? Saying is negative, makes us feel bad about selves.

I say maybe we should just confess what Eva did, hope for mercy from Greenway.

Pam says no, no: went on-line today: releasing SGs = felony (!). Does not feel they would prosecute eight-year-old, but still. If we confess, this goes on Eva's record? Eva required to get counseling? This goes on her record? Eva feels: I am bad kid? Starts erring on side of bad, hanging out with rough crowd, looking askance at whole notion of achievement, fails to live up to full potential, all because of one mistake she made when little girl?

No.

Cannot take chance.

Pam and I discuss, agree: must be like sin-eaters who, in ancient times, ate sin. Or bodies of sinners? Ate meals off bodies of sinners who had died? Cannot exactly recall what sin-eaters did. But Pam and I agree: are going to be like sin-eaters in sense of: will err on side of protecting Eva, keep cops in dark at all costs, break law as req'd.

Pam asks: am I still writing in book? Isn't book = legal document? Have I written in book about Eva, about Eva's role in? Wouldn't book prove us guilty of obstruction of justice? Couldn't they subpoena book? Shouldn't I stop writing in book, expunge questionable pages? Hide book? Drop book down hole I kicked in wall the other day? Better yet, destroy book?

Tell Pam I love writing in book, do not want to stop writing in book, destroy book.

Pam: Well, it's up to you. But to me? It's not worth it.

Pam smart. Pam excellent judge of situations. Am thinking this over. (If book goes silent, future reader will know I (once again!) decided Pam = right.)

My guess, my hope: cops have many similar cases, we are small fish, our case = low priority, all this will soon fade away.

(Oct. 8)

Wrong. Wrong again. This not fading away.

Will explain.

Worked all day.

Was normal boring day.

Can future reader imagine how agonizing it was to plod through normal boring day when all I wanted to do was rush home, strategize w/Pam re. Eva situation, pluck Eva from school, give Eva big hug, tell Eva all will be well, assure Eva that, even though we do not approve of what she did, she will always be our girl, will always be apple of our eye(s)?

But in this life, dad must do what dad must do.

Stuck out whole day.

Then usual drive home: zone of used car dealerships, zone of quarry, long stretch of highway looking down on bad apartments w/clothes on lines, relatively pastoral stretch with pioneer graveyard, former mall gone belly-up.

Then our little house + sad empty yard.

Guy standing at back gate.

Went over, had chat with guy.

Guy = Jerry. Is detective (!) assigned to our case. Activists = big priority for city, he says, mayor determined to send strong signal (!). Says he knows we are behind eight-ball in terms of money, feels shysters at Greenway deserve to be boiled in oil. Is man of limited means himself, he says, is family man, knows how upset he would be if he owed big faceless corporation $8600. But no worries, he is on it. Will not rest until activists found. Has low regard for activists. Activists think they are doing noble thing? Are not. SGs become illegal immigrants, take jobs away from "legit Americans." Jerry very much against. Jerry's father came from Ireland on boat, vomiting whole trip, then filled out required forms. This = proper way, Jerry feels.

Ha ha, he says.

Smiles, wipes mouth.

Jerry a talker. Before he became cop, was teacher. Is so glad to not be teaching anymore. His students brats. Brattier every year. For last few years, was just biding his time, waiting to be knifed or shot by some brat. Things got worse as kids got darker. If I know what he means. Has nothing against dark people but does have something against dark people who refuse to work and learn language and insist on pulling mean pranks on teachers. When he was kid, would never have dreamed of putting small baby frog in Diet Coke of one of most dedicated teachers on staff. Was almost certainly dark kid who did it, since nearly all his kids dark kids. Was never personally knifed, but is sure he would have been, eventually, by some dark kid or other. For any kid nervy enough to put frog in teacher's drink, sky is limit, i.e., stabbing = next logical step.

Kids just kids, I say.

Yes and no, Jerry says. Kids = future adults. What is good for goose is good for gander. Once saw film re. baby lion allowed to run rampant: lion grew up, ate own owner. Therefore, firm hand tantamount w/ kids.

Jerry lonely lately, he says. His wife recently died. Did not plan on her dying first. She was always healthy one. Now he is little bit lost. Wife was just wisp of thing even at best.

Toward end, she was almost not there. Is never in big rush to get home. Home so quiet since wife gone. Has no grandkids, as never had kids, as wife had questionable eggs.

Hence will have plenty of time to dedicate to our case.

Something fishy here, Jerry says. Does not look like typical activist job. Activists will normally leave calling card: Semplica Rots in Hell leaves single red flag. Women4Women leaves manifesto + tape recording of SGs listing things family did to offend/annoy SGs during time in yard. Activists will often have doctor as part of team, to remove microline before SGs get in van. Yet cops found microline drag marks near our gate, indicating SGs escaped on foot, microline still in?

Does not add up.

Jerry smells rat.

But not to worry, Jerry says: he is "here for duration."

For now, will sit in yard awhile. This how he sometimes proceeds: will get "right into head of perp."

Jerry hacks, hobbles away into yard.

Go inside. Tell Pam all.

Pam and I stand at window watching Jerry.

Thomas: Who is that?

Me: Just a guy.

Pam: Don't go out there. Don't talk to him or anything like that.

Lilly: He's in our yard but we're not allowed to talk to him?

Me: Yes. Correct.

Is nearly midnight as I write. Jerry still in yard (!). Jerry smoking, Jerry humming same annoying four-note phrase over and over. Can hear him from spare room + smell his smoke. Would like to go down, order Jerry from yard. Say: Jerry, this = our yard. Our kids sleeping, they have school tomorrow, if you wake them with your humming, they will have rough/sleepy day at school. Also, Jerry, we do not allow smoking in or near house.

Yet cannot do.

Must not alienate Jerry in slightest way.

God.

Household in freefall, future reader. Everything chaotic. Kids, feeling tension, fighting all day. After dinner, Pam caught kids watching "I, Gropius," (forbidden) = show where guy decides which girl to date based on feeling girls' breasts through screen with two holes. (Do not actually show breasts. Just guy's expressions as he feels them and girl's expression as he feels them and girl's expression as guy announces his rating. Still: bad show.) Pam blew up at kids: We are in most difficult period ever for family, this how they behave?

When kids born, Pam and I dropped everything (youthful dreams of travel, adventure, etc., etc.) to be good parents. Has not been exciting life. Has been much drudgery. Many nights, tasks undone, have stayed up late, exhausted, doing tasks. On many occasions, disheveled + tired, baby-poop and/or -vomit on our shirt or blouse, one of us has stood smiling wearily/angrily at camera being held by other, hair shaggy because haircuts expensive, unfashionable glasses slipping down noses because never had time to get glasses tightened.

And after all that, look where we are.

Is unfortunate.

Just now went down hall to check on kids. Thomas sleeping w/Ferber. This not allowed. Eva in bed w/Lilly. This not allowed. Eva, source of all mayhem, sleeping like baby.

Felt like waking Eva, telling Eva all will be well, she has good heart, is just young + confused.

Did not do.

Eva needs rest.

On Lilly's desk: poster Lilly was working on for "Favorite Things Day" at school. Poster = photo of each SG, plus map of home country, plus stories Lilly apparently got during interview (!) with each: Gwen (Moldova) = very tough, due to Moldovian youth: used bloody sheets found in trash + duct tape to make soccer ball, then, after much practice with bloody-sheet ball, nearly made Olympic team (!). Betty (Philippines) has daughter who, when swimming, will sometimes hitch ride on shell of sea turtle. Lisa (Somalia) once saw lion on roof of her uncle's "mini-lorry." Tami (Laos) had pet water buffalo, water buffalo stepped on her foot, now Tami must wear special shoe. "Fun Fact": their names (Betty, Tami, et al.) not their real names. These = SG names, given by Greenway at time of arrival. "Tami" = Januka = "happy ray of sun." "Betty" = Nenita = "blessed-beloved." "Gwen" = Evgenia. (Does not know what her name means.) "Lisa" = Ayan = "happy traveler."

SGs very much on my mind tonight, future reader.

Where are they now? Why did they go?

Just do not get.

Letter comes, family celebrates, girl sheds tears, stoically packs bag, thinks: must go, am family's only hope. Puts on brave face, promises she will return as soon as contract complete. Her mother feels, father feels: we cannot let her go. But they do. They must.

Whole town walks girl to train station/bus station/ferry stop? Group rides in brightly colored van to tiny regional airport? More tears, more vows. As train/ferry/plane pulls away, she takes last fond look at surrounding hills/river/quarry/shacks, whatever, i.e., all she has ever known of world, saying to self: be not afraid, you will return, & return in victory, w/big bag of gifts, etc, etc.

And now?

No money, no papers. Who will remove microline? Who will give her job? When going for job, must fix hair so as to hide scars at Insertion Points. When will she ever see home + family again? Why would she do? Why would she ruin it all, leave our yard? Could have had nice long run w/us. What in the world was she seeking? What could she want so much, that would make her pull such desperate stunt?

Jerry just now left for night.

Empty rack out in yard, looking strange in moonlight.

Note to self: call Greenway, have them take ugly thing away.

HOME

1.

Like in the old days, I came out of the dry creek behind the house and did my little tap on the kitchen window.

"Get in here, you," Ma said.

Inside were piles of newspaper on the stove and piles of magazines on the stairs and a big wad of hangers sticking out of the broken oven. All of that was as usual. New was: a water stain the shape of a cat head above the fridge and the old orange rug rolled up halfway.

"Still ain't no beeping cleaning lady," Ma said.

I looked at her funny.

" 'Beeping?' " I said.

"Beep you," she said. "They been on my case at work."

It was true Ma had a pretty good potty mouth. And was working at a church now, so.

We stood there looking at each other.

Then some guy came tromping down the stairs: older than Ma even, in just boxers and hiking boots and a winter cap, long ponytail hanging out the back.

"Who's this?" he said.

"My son," Ma said shyly. "Mikey, this is Harris."

"What's your worst thing you ever did over there?" Harris said.

"What happened to Alberto?" I said.

"Alberto flew the coop," Ma said.

"Alberto showed his ass," Harris said.

"I hold nothing against that beeper," Ma said.

"I hold a lot against that fucker," Harris said. "Including he owes me ten bucks."

"Harris ain't dealing with his potty mouth," Ma said.

"She's only doing it because of work," Harris explained.

"Harris don't work," Ma said.

"Well, if I did work, it wouldn't be at a place that tells me how I can talk," Harris said. "It would be at a place that lets me talk how I like. A place that accepts me for who I am. That's the kind of place I'd be willing to work."

"There ain't many of that kind of place," Ma said.

"Places that let me talk how I want?" Harris said. "Or places that accept me for who I am?"

"Places you'd be willing to work," Ma said.

"How long's he staying?" Harris said.

"Long as he wants," Ma said.

"My house is your house," Harris said to me.

"It ain't your house," Ma said.

"Give the kid some food at least," Harris said.

"I will but it ain't your idea," Ma said, and shooed us out of the kitchen.

"Great lady," Harris said. "Had my eyes on her for years. Then Alberto split. That I don't get. You got a great lady in your life, the lady gets sick, you split?"

"Ma's sick?" I said.

"She didn't tell you?" he said.

He grimaced, made his hand into a fist, put it upside his head.

"Lump," he said. "But you didn't hear it from me."

Ma was singing now in the kitchen.

"I hope you're at least making bacon," Harris called out. "A kid comes home deserves some frigging bacon."

"Why not stay out of it?" Ma called back. "You just met him."

"I love him like my own son," Harris said.

"What a ridiculous statement," Ma said. "You hate your son."

"I hate both my sons," Harris said.

"And you'd hate your daughter if you ever meet her," Ma said.

Harris beamed, as if touched that Ma knew him well enough to know he would inevitably hate any child he fathered.

Ma came in with some bacon and eggs on a saucer.

"Might be a hair in it," she said. "Lately it's like I'm beeping shedding."

"You are certainly welcome," Harris said.

"You didn't beeping do nothing!" Ma said. "Don't take credit. Go in there and do the dishes. That would help."

"I can't do dishes and you know that," Harris said. "On account of my rash."

"He gets a rash from water," Ma said. "Ask him why he can't dry."

"On account of my back," Harris said.

"He's the King of If," Ma said. "What he ain't is King of Actually Do."

"Soon as he leaves I'll show you what I'm king of," Harris said.

"Oh, Harris, that is too much, that is truly disgusting," Ma said.

Harris raised both hands over his head like: Winner and still champ.

"We'll put you in your old room," Ma said.

2.

On my bed was a hunting bow and a purple Halloween cape
with built-in ghost face.

"That's Harris's beep," Ma said.

"Ma," I said. "Harris told me."

I made my hand into a fist, put it upside my head.

She gave me a blank look.

"Or maybe I didn't understand him right," I said. "Lump?
He said you've got a—"

"Or maybe he's a big beeping liar," she said. "He makes
up crazy beep about me all the time. It's like his hobby. He
told the mailman I had a fake leg. He told Eileen at the deli
one of my eyes was glass. He told the guy at the hardware I
get fainting dealies and froth at the mouth whenever I get
mad. Now that guy's always rushing me outta there."

To show how fine she was, Ma did a jumping jack.

Harris was clomping upstairs.

"I won't tell you told about the lump," Ma said. "You
don't tell I told about him being a liar."

Now this was starting to seem like the old days.

"Ma," I said, "where are Renee and Ryan living?"

"Uh," Ma said.

"They got a sweet place over there," Harris said. "Rolling
in the dough."

"I'm not sure that's the best idea," Ma said.

"Your ma thinks Ryan's a hitter," Harris said.

"Ryan is a hitter," Ma said. "I can always tell a hitter."

"He hits?" I said. "He hits Renee?"

"You didn't hear it from me," Ma said.

"He better not start hitting that baby," Harris said. "Sweet little Martney. Kid's super-cute."

"Although what the beep kinda name is that?" Ma said. "I told Renee that. I said that."

"Is that a boy or a girl name?" Harris said.

"What the beep you talking about?" Ma said. "You seen it. You held it."

"Looks like a elf," Harris said.

"But girl or boy elf?" Ma said. "Watch. He really don't know."

"Well, it was wearing green," Harris said. "So that don't help me."

"Think," Ma said. "What did we buy it?"

"You'd think I'd know boy or girl," Harris said. "It being my freaking grandkid."

"It ain't your grandkid," Ma said. "We bought it a boat."

"A boat could be for boys or girls," Harris said. "Don't be prejudice. A girl can love a boat. Just like a boy can love a doll. Or a bra."

"Well, we didn't buy it a doll or a bra," Ma said. "We bought it a boat."

I went downstairs, got the phone book. Renee and Ryan lived over on Lincoln. 27 Lincoln.

3.

27 Lincoln was in the good part of downtown.

I couldn't believe the house. Couldn't believe the turrets. The back gate was redwood and opened so smooth, like the hinge was hydraulic.

Couldn't believe the yard.

I squatted in some bushes by the screened-in porch. Inside, some people were talking: Renee, Ryan, Ryan's parents, sounded like. Ryan's parents had sonorous/confident voices that seemed to have been fabricated out of previous, less sonorous/confident voices by means of sudden money.

"Say what you will about Lon Brewster," Ryan's dad said. "But Lon came out and retrieved me from Feldspar that time I had a flat."

"In that ridiculous broiling heat," said Ryan's mom.

"And not a word of complaint," said Ryan's dad. "A completely charming person."

"Almost as charming—or so you told me—as the Flemings," she said.

"And the Flemings are awfully charming," he said.

"And the good they do!" she said. "They flew a planeload of babies over here."

"Russian babies," he said. "With harelips."

"Soon as the babies arrived, they were whisked into various operating rooms all around the country," she said. "And who paid?"

"The Flemings," he said.

"Didn't they also set aside some money for college?" she said. "For the Russians?"

"Those kids went from being disabled in a collapsing nation to being set for life in the greatest country in the world," he said. "And who did this? A corporation? The government?"

"One private couple," she said.

"A truly visionary pair of folks," he said.

There was a long admiring pause.

"Although you'd never know it by how harshly he speaks to her," she said.

"Well, she can be awfully harsh with him as well," he said.

"Sometimes it's just him being harsh with her and her being harsh right back," she said.

"It's like the chicken or the egg," he said.

"Only with harshness," she said.

"Still, you can't help but love the Flemings," he said.

"We should be so wonderful," she said. "When was the last time we rescued a Russian baby?"

"Well, we do all right," he said. "We can't afford to fly a bunch of Russian babies over here, but I think, in our own limited way, we do just fine."

"We can't even fly over one Russian," she said. "Even a Canadian baby with a harelip would be beyond our means."

"We could probably drive up there and pick one up," he said. "But then what? We can't afford the surgery and can't afford the college. So the baby's just sitting here, in America instead of Canada, still with the lip issue."

"Did we tell you kids?" she said. "We're adding five shops. Five shops around the tri-city area. Each with a fountain."

"That's great, Mom," Ryan said.

"That is so great," Renee said.

"And maybe, if those five shops do well, we can open another three or four shops and, at that time, revisit this whole Russian-harelip issue," Ryan's father said.

"You guys continue to amaze," Ryan said.

Renee stepped out with the baby.

"I'm going to step out with the baby," she said.

4.

The baby had taken its toll. Renee seemed wider, less peppy. Also paler, like someone had run a color-leaching beam over her face and hair.

The baby did look like an elf.

The elf-baby looked at a bird, pointed at the bird.

"Bird," said Renee.

The elf-baby looked at their insane pool.

"For swimming," said Renee. "But not yet. Not yet, right?"

The elf-baby looked at the sky.

"Clouds," Renee said. "Clouds make rain."

It was like the baby was demanding, with its eyes: Hurry up, tell me what all this shit is, so I can master it, open a few shops.

The baby looked at me.

Renee nearly dropped the baby.

"Mike, Mikey, holy shit," she said.

Then she seemed to remember something and hustled back to the porch door.

"Rye?" she called. "Rye-King? Can you come get the Mart-Heart?"

Ryan took the baby.

"Love you," I heard him say.

"Love you more," she said.

Then she came back, no baby.

"I call him Rye-King," she said, blushing.

"I heard that," I said.

"Mikey," she said. "Did you do it?"

"Can I come in?" I said.

"Not today," she said. "Tomorrow. No, Thursday. His folks leave Wednesday. Come over Thursday, we'll hash it all out."

"Hash what out?" I said.

"Whether you can come in," she said.

"I didn't realize that was a question," I said.

"Did you?" she said. "Do it?"

"Ryan seems nice," I said.

"Oh God," she said. "Literally the nicest human being I have ever known."

"Except when he's hitting," I said.

"When what?" she said.

"Ma told me," I said.

"Told you what?" she said. "That Ryan hits? Hits me? Ma said that?"

"Don't tell her I told," I said, a little panicked, as of old.

"Ma's deranged," she said. "Ma's out of her frigging mind. Ma *would* say that. You know who's gonna get hit? Ma. By me."

"Why didn't you write me about Ma?" I said.

"What about her?" she said suspiciously.

"She's sick?" I said.

"She told you?" she said.

I made a fist and held it upside my head.

"What's that?" she said.

"A lump?" I said.

"Ma doesn't have a lump," she said. "She's got a fucked-up heart. Who told you she's got a lump?"

"Harris," I said.

"Oh, Harris, perfect," she said.

Inside the house, the baby started crying.

"Go," Renee said. "We'll talk Thursday. But first."

She took my face in her hands and turned my head so I was looking in the window at Ryan, who was heating a bottle at the kitchen sink.

"Does that look like a hitter?" she said.

"No," I said.

And it didn't. Not at all.

"Jesus," I said. "Does anybody tell the truth around here?"

"I do," she said. "You do."

I looked at her and for a minute she was eight and I was ten and we were hiding in the doghouse while Ma and Dad and Aunt Toni, on mushrooms, trashed the patio.

"Mikey," she said. "I need to know. Did you do it?"

I jerked my face out of her hands, turned, went.

"Go see your own wife, doofus!" she shouted after me. "Go see your own babies."

5.

Ma was on the front lawn, screaming at this low-slung fat guy. Harris was looming in the background, now and then hitting or kicking something to show how scary he could get when enraged.

"This is my son!" Ma said. "Who served. Who just came home. And this is how you do us?"

"I'm grateful for your service," the man said to me.

Harris kicked the metal garbage can.

"Will you please tell him to stop doing that?" the man said.

"He has no control over me when I'm mad," Harris said. "No one does."

"Do you think I like this?" the man said. "She hasn't paid rent in four months."

"Three," Ma said.

"This is how you treat the family of a hero?" Harris said. "He's over there fighting and you're over here abusing his mother?"

"Friend, excuse me, I'm not abusing," the man said. "This is evicting. If she'd paid her rent and I was evicting, that would be abusing."

"And here I work for a beeping church!" Ma shouted.

The man, though low-slung and fat, was admirably bold. He went inside the house and came out carrying the TV with a bored look on his face, like it was his TV and he preferred it in the yard.

"No," I said.

"I appreciate your service," he said.

I took him by the shirt. I was, by this time, good at taking people by their shirts, looking them in the eye, speaking directly.

"Whose house is this?" I said.

"Mine," he said.

I put my foot behind him, dropped him on the grass.

"Go easy," Harris said.

"That was easy," I said, and carried the TV back inside.

6.

That night the sheriff arrived with some movers, who emptied the house onto the lawn.

I saw them coming and went out the back door and watched it all from High Street, sitting in the deer stand behind the Nestons'.

Ma was out there, head in hands, weaving in and out of her heaped-up crap. It was both melodramatic and not. I mean, when Ma feels something deeply, that's what she does: melodrama. Which makes it, I guess, not melodrama?

Something had been happening to me lately where a plan would start flowing directly down to my hands and feet. When that happened, I knew to trust it. My face would get hot and I'd feel sort of like, Go, go, go.

It had served me well, mostly.

Now the plan flowing down was: grab Ma, push her inside, make her sit, round up Harris, make him sit, torch the place, or at least make the first motions of torching the place, to get their attention, make them act their age.

I flew down the hill, pushed Ma inside, sat her on the stairs, grabbed Harris by the shirt, put my foot behind him, dropped him to the floor. Then held a match to the carpet on the stairs and, once it started burning, raised a finger, like, Quiet, through me runs the power of recent dark experience.

They were both so scared they weren't talking at all, which made me feel the kind of shame you know you're not going to cure by saying sorry, and where the only thing to do is: go out, get more shame.

I stomped the carpet fire out and went over to Gleason Street, where Joy and the babies were living with Asshole.

7.

What a kick in the head: their place was even nicer than Renee's.

The house was dark. There were three cars in the driveway. Which meant that they were all home and in bed.

I stood thinking about that a bit.

Then walked back downtown and into a store. I guess it was a store. Although I couldn't tell what they were selling. On yellow counters lit from within were these heavy blue-plastic tags. I picked one up. On it was the word "MiiVOX-MAX."

"What is it?" I said.

"It's more like what's it for, is how I'd say it," this kid said.

"What's it for?" I said.

"Actually," he said, "this is probably more the one for you."

He handed me an identical tag but with the word "Mii-VOXMIN" on it.

Another kid came over with espresso and cookies.

I put down the MiiVOXMIN tag and picked up the Mii-VOXMAX tag.

"How much?" I said.

"You mean money?" he said.

"What does it do?" I said.

"Well, if you're asking is it data repository or information-hierarchy domain?" he said. "The answer to that would be: yes and no."

They were sweet. Not a line on their faces. When I say they were kids, I mean they were about my age.

"I've been away a long time," I said.

"Welcome back," the first kid said.

"Where were you?" the second one said.

"At the war?" I said, in the most insulting voice I could muster. "Maybe you've heard of it?"

"I have," the first one said respectfully. "Thank you for your service."

"Which one?" the second one said. "Aren't there two?"

"Didn't they just call one off?" the first one said.

"My cousin's there," the second said. "At one of them. At least I think he is. I know he was supposed to go. We were never that close."

"Anyway, thanks," the first one said, and put out his hand, and I shook it.

"I wasn't for it," the second one said. "But I know it wasn't your deal."

"Well," I said. "It kind of was."

"You *weren't* for it or *aren't* for it?" the first said to the second.

"Both," the second one said. "Although is it still going?"

"Which one?" the first one said.

"Is the one you were at still going?" the second one asked me.

"Yes," I said.

"Better or worse, do you think?" the first one said. "Like, in your view, are we winning? Oh, what am I doing? I don't actually care, that's what's so funny about it!"

"Anyway," the second one said, and held out his hand, and I shook it.

They were so nice and accepting and unsuspicious—they were so *for* me—that I walked out smiling and was about a block away before I realized I was still holding MiiVOX-MAX. I got under a streetlight and had a look. It seemed like just a plastic tag. Like, if you wanted MiiVOXMAX, you handed in that tag, and someone went and got MiiVOXMAX for you, whatever it was.

8.

Asshole answered the door.

His actual name was Evan. We'd gone to school together. I had a vague memory of him in an Indian headdress, racing down a hallway.

"Mike," he said.

"Can I come in?" I said.

"I think I have to say no to that," he said.

"I'd like to see the kids," I said.

"Past midnight," he said.

I had a pretty good idea he was lying. Were stores open past midnight? Still, the moon was high and there was something moist and sad in the air that seemed to be saying, Well, it's not *early*.

"Tomorrow?" I said.

"Would that be okay for you?" he said. "After I get home from work?"

I saw we'd agreed to play it reasonable. One way we were playing it reasonable was saying everything like a question.

"Around six?" I said.

"Does six work for you?" he said.

The weird part was I'd never actually seen the two of them together. The wife back there in his bed could have been someone else entirely.

"I know this isn't easy," he said.

"You fucked me," I said.

"I would respectfully disagree with that," he said.

"No doubt," I said.

"I didn't fuck you and she didn't," he said. "It was a challenging circumstance for all involved."

"More challenging for some than for others," I said. "Would you give me that much?"

"Are we being honest?" he said. "Or tiptoeing around conflict?"

"Honest," I said, and his face did this thing that, for a minute, made me like him again.

"It was hard for me because I felt like a shit," he said. "It was hard for her because she felt like a shit. It was hard for us because while feeling like shits we were also feeling all the other things we were feeling, which, I assure you, were and are as real as anything, a total blessing, if I can say it that way."

At that point, I started feeling like a chump, like I was being held down by a bunch of guys so another guy could come over and put his New Age fist up my ass while explaining that having his fist up my ass was far from his first choice and was actually making him feel conflicted.

"Six o'clock," I said.

"Six o'clock's perfect," he said. "Luckily, I'm on flextime."

"You don't need to be here," I said.

"If you were me and I was you, would you maybe feel you might somewhat need to be here?" he said.

One car was a Saab and one an Escalade and the third a newer Saab, with two baby seats in it and a stuffed clown I was not familiar with.

Three cars for two grown-ups, I thought. What a country. What a couple selfish dicks my wife and her new husband were. I could see that, over the years, my babies would slowly transform into selfish-dick babies, then selfish-dick toddlers, kids, teenagers, and adults, with me all that time skulking around like some unclean suspect uncle.

That part of town was full of castles. Inside one was a couple embracing. Inside another a woman had like nine million little Christmas houses out on a table, like she was taking inventory. Across the river the castles got smaller. By our part of town, the houses were like peasant huts. Inside one peasant hut were five kids standing perfectly still on the back of a couch. Then they all leapt off at once and their dogs went crazy.

9.

Ma's house was empty. Ma and Harris were sitting on the floor in the living room, making phone calls, trying to find somewhere to go.

"What time is it?" I said.

Ma looked up at where the clock used to be.

"The clock's on the sidewalk," she said.

I went out. The clock was under a coat. It was ten. Evan had fucked me. I considered going back, demanding to see the kids, but by the time I got there it would be eleven and he'd still have a decent point re the lateness of the hour.

The sheriff walked in.

"Don't get up," he said to Ma.

Ma got up.

"Get up," he said to me.

I stayed sitting.

"You the one who threw down Mr. Klees?" the sheriff said.

"He's just back from the war," Ma said.

"Thank you for your service," the sheriff said. "Might I ask you to refrain from throwing people down in the future?"

"He also threw me down," Harris said.

"My thing is I don't want to go around arresting veterans," the sheriff said. "I myself am a veteran. So if you help me, by not throwing anyone else down, I'll help you. By not arresting you. Deal?"

"He was also going to burn the house down," Ma said.

"I wouldn't recommend burning anything down," the sheriff said.

"He ain't himself," Ma said. "I mean, look at him."

The sheriff had never seen me before, but it was like admitting he had no basis for assessing how I looked would have been a professional embarrassment.

"He does look tired," the sheriff said.

"Plenty strong, though," Harris said. "Threw me right down."

"Where are you folks off to tomorrow?" the sheriff said.

"Suggestions?" Ma said.

"A friend, a family member?" the sheriff said.

"Renee's," I said.

"Failing that, the shelter on Fristen?" the sheriff said.

"One thing I am not doing is going to Renee's," Ma said.

"Everyone in that house is too high and mighty. They already think of us as low."

"Well, we are low," said Harris. "Compared to them."

"The other thing I'm not doing is going to any beeping shelter," Ma said. "They got crabs at shelters."

"When we first started dating I had crabs from that shelter," Harris said helpfully.

"I'm sorry this is happening," the sheriff said. "Everything's backwards and inverted."

"I'll say," Ma said. "Here I work for a church and my son's a hero. With a Silver Star. Dragged a marine out by the beeping foot. We got the letter. And where am I? Out on the street."

The sheriff had switched off and was waiting to make his break for the door and get back to whatever was real to him.

"Find someplace to live, folks," he advised genially as he left.

Harris and I dragged two mattresses back in. They still had the sheets and blankets on and all. But the sheet on their mattress had grass stains on one edge and the pillows smelled like mud.

Then we spent a long night in the bare house.

10.

In the morning Ma called some ladies she'd known as a young mother, but one had a disk out and another had cancer and a third had twins who'd both just been diagnosed manic-depressive.

In the light of day Harris braved up again.

"So this court-martial thing," he said. "Was that the worst thing you ever did? Or was there worse things, which you did but just didn't get caught?"

"They cleared him of that," Ma said tersely.

"Well, they cleared me of breaking and entering that time," Harris said.

"Anyways, how is this any of your business?" Ma said.

"Probably he wants to talk," Harris said. "Get some air in there. Good for the soul."

"Look at his face, Har," Ma said.

Harris looked at my face.

"Sorry I mentioned it," he said.

Then the sheriff was back. He made me and Harris drag the mattresses out. On the porch we watched him padlock the door.

"Eighteen years you have been my dear home," Ma said, possibly imitating some Sioux from a movie.

"You're going to want to get a van over here," the sheriff said.

"My son served in the war," Ma said. "And look how you're doing me."

"I'm the same guy that was here yesterday," the sheriff said, and for some reason framed his face with his hands. "Remember me? You told me that already. I thanked him for his service. Call a van. Or your shit's going to the dump."

"See how they treat a lady works at a church," Ma said.

Ma and Harris picked through their crap, found a suitcase, filled the suitcase with clothes.

Then we drove to Renee's.

My feeling was, Oh, this will be funny.

11.

Although yes and no. That was just one of my feelings.

Another was, Oh, Ma, I remember when you were young and wore your hair in braids and I would have died to see you sink so low.

Another was, You crazy old broad, you narced me out last night. What was up with that?

Another was, Mom, Mommy, let me kneel at your feet and tell you what me and Smelton and Ricky G. did at Al-Raz, and then you stroke my hair and tell me anybody would've done the exact same thing.

As we crossed the Roll Creek Bridge I could see that Ma was feeling, Just let that Renee deny me, I will hand that little beep her beeping beep on a platter.

But then, bango, by the time we got to the far side and the air had gone from river-cool to regular again, her face had changed to: Oh, God, if Renee denies me in front of Ryan's parents and they once again find me trash, I will die, I will simply die.

12.

Renee did deny her in front of Ryan's parents, who did find her trash.

But she didn't die.

You should have seen their faces as we walked in.

Renee looked stricken. Ryan looked stricken. Ryan's mom and dad were trying so hard not to look stricken that they kept knocking things over. A vase went down as Ryan's dad blundered forward trying to look chipper/welcoming. Ryan's mom lurched into a painting and ended up holding it in her crossed red-sweatered arms.

"Is this the baby?" I said.

Ma turned on me again.

"What do you think it is?" she said. "A midget that can't talk?"

"This is Martney, yes," Renee said, holding the baby out to me.

Ryan cleared his throat, shot Renee a look like, I thought we'd discussed this, Love Muffin.

Renee changed the baby's course, swerved it up, like if she held it high enough, that would negate the need for me to hold it, it being so close to the overhead light and all.

Which hurt.

"Fuck it," I said. "What do you think I'm going to do?"

"Please don't say 'fuck' in our home," Ryan said.

"Please don't tell my son what the beep he can beeping say," Ma said. "Him being in the war and all."

"Thank you for your service," Ryan's dad said.

"We can easily go to a hotel," Ryan's mom said.

"You are not going to any hotel, Mom," Ryan said. "They can go to a hotel."

"We're not going to a hotel," Ma said.

"You can easily go to a hotel, Mother. You love a good hotel," Renee said. "Especially when we're paying."

Even Harris was nervous.

"A hotel sounds lovely," he said. "It's been many a day since I reclined in a nice place of that nature as a hotel."

"You'd send your own mother, who works for a church, along with your brother, a Silver Star hero just home from the war, to some fleabag?" Ma said.

"Yes," Renee said.

"Can I at least hold the baby?" I said.

"Not on my watch," Ryan said.

"Jane and I would like you to know how much we supported, and still do support, your mission," Ryan's father said.

"A lot of people don't know how many schools you fellows built over there," Ryan's mother said.

"People tend to focus on the negative," Ryan's dad said.

"What's that proverb?" Ryan's mother said. "To make something or other, you first have to break a lot of something or other?"

"I think he could hold the baby," said Renee. "I mean, we're standing right here."

Ryan winced, shook his head.

The baby writhed, like it too believed its fate was being decided.

Having all these people think I was going to hurt the baby made me imagine hurting the baby. Did imagining hurting the baby mean that I *would* hurt the baby? Did I *want* to hurt the baby? No, Jesus. But: Did the fact that I had no intention of hurting the baby mean that I wouldn't, when push came to shove, hurt the baby? Had I, in the recent past, had the experience of having no intention of doing Activity A, then suddenly finding myself right in the middle of doing Activity A?

"I don't want to hold the baby," I said.

"I appreciate that," Ryan said. "That's cool of you."

"I want to hold this pitcher," I said, and picked up a pitcher and held it like a baby, with the lemonade spilling out of it, and, once the lemonade was pooling nicely on the hardwood floor, spiked the pitcher down.

"You really hurt my feelings!" I said.

Then was out on the sidewalk, walking fast.

13.

Then was back in that store.

Two different guys were there, younger than the earlier two. They might have been high schoolers. I handed over the MiiVOXMAX tag.

"Oh shit, snap!" the one guy said. "We were wondering where that was."

"We were about to call it in," the other guy said, bringing over espresso and cookies.

"Is it valuable?" I said.

"Ha, oh, boy," the first one said, and got some kind of special cloth from under the counter and dusted the tag off and put it back on display.

"What is it?" I said.

"It's more like what's it for, is how I'd say it," the first guy said.

"What's it for?" I said.

"This might be more in your line," he said and handed me the MiiVOXMIN tag.

"I've been away a long time," I said.

"Us, too," the second kid said.

"We just got out of the army," the first kid said.

Then we all took turns saying where we'd been.

Turned out me and the first guy had been in basically the same place.

"Wait, so were you at Al-Raz?" I said.

"I was totally at Al-Raz," the first guy said.

"I was never in the shit, I admit it," the second guy said. "Although I did once run over a dog with a forklift."

I asked the first guy if he remembered the baby goat, the pocked wall, the crying toddler, the dark arched doorway, the doves that suddenly exploded out from under that peeling gray eave.

"I wasn't over by that," he said. "I was more over by the river and the upside-down boat and that little family all in red that kept turning up everywhere you looked?"

I knew exactly where he'd been. It was unbelievable how many times, pre- and post-exploding doves, I'd caught sight, on the horizon, down by the river, of some imploring or crouching or fleeing figure in red.

"It ended up cool with that dog, though," the second guy said. "He lived and all. By the time I left, he'd be like riding right up alongside me in the forklift."

A family of nine Indian-Americans came in, and the second guy went over to them with the espresso and cookies.

"Al-Raz, wow," I said, in an exploratory way.

"For me?" the first guy said. "Al-Raz was the worst day of the whole deal."

"Yes, me too, exactly," I said.

"I fucked up big-time at Al-Raz," he said.

Suddenly I found I couldn't breathe.

"My boy Melvin?" he said. "Got a chunk of shrapnel right in the groin. Because of me. I waited too long to call it in. There was this like lady party going on right nearby? About fifteen gals in this corner store. And kids with them. So I waited. Too bad for Melvin. For Melvin's groin."

Now he was waiting for me to tell the fucked-up thing I'd done.

I put down MiiVOXMIN, picked it up, put it down.

"Melvin's okay, though," he said, and did a little two-finger tap on his own groin. "He's home, you know, in grad school. He's fucking, apparently."

"Glad to hear it," I said. "Probably he even sometimes rides up alongside you in the forklift."

"Sorry?" he said.

I looked at the clock on the wall. It didn't seem to have any hands. It was just a moving pattern of yellow and white.

"Do you know what time it is?" I said.

The guy looked up at the clock.

"Six," he said.

14.

Out on the street I found a pay phone and called Renee.

"I'm sorry," I said. "Sorry about that pitcher."

"Yeah, well," she said in her non-fancy voice. "You're gonna buy me a new one."

I could hear she was trying to make up.

"No," I said. "I won't be doing that."

"Where are you, Mikey?" she said.

"Nowhere," I said.

"Where are you going?" she said.

"Home," I said and hung up.

15.

Coming up Gleason, I had that feeling. My hands and feet didn't know exactly what they wanted, but they were trending toward: push past whatever/whoever blocks you, get inside, start wrecking shit by throwing it around, shout out whatever's in your mind, see what happens.

I was on a like shame slide. You know what I mean? Once, back in high school, this guy paid me to clean some gunk out of his pond. You snagged the gunk with a rake, then rake-hurled it. At one point, the top of my rake flew into the gunk pile. When I went to retrieve it, there were like a million tadpoles, dead and dying, at whatever age they are when they've got those swollen bellies like little pregnant ladies. What the dead and dying had in common was: their tender white underbellies had been torn open by the gunk suddenly crashing down on them from on high. The difference was: the dying were the ones doing the mad fear gesticulating.

I tried to save a few, but they were so tender all I did by handling them was torture them worse.

Maybe someone could've said to the guy who'd hired me, "Uh, I have to stop now, I feel bad for killing so many tadpoles." But I couldn't. So I kept on rake-hurling.

With each rake hurl I thought, I'm making more bloody bellies.

The fact that I kept rake-hurling started making me mad at the frogs.

It was like either: (A) I was a terrible guy who was knowingly doing this rotten thing over and over, or (B) it wasn't so rotten, really, just normal, and the way to confirm it was normal was to keep doing it, over and over.

Years later, at Al-Raz, it was a familiar feeling.

Here was the house.

Here was the house where they cooked, laughed, fucked. Here was the house that, in the future, when my name came up, would get all hushed, and Joy would be like, "Although Evan is no, not your real daddy, me and Daddy Evan feel you don't need to be around Daddy Mike all that much, because what me and Daddy Evan really care about is you two growing up strong and healthy, and sometimes mommies and daddies need to make a special atmosphere in which that can happen."

I looked for the three cars in the driveway. Three cars meant: all home. Did I want all home? I did. I wanted all, even the babies, to see and participate and be sorry for what had happened to me.

But instead of three cars in the driveway there were five.

Evan was on the porch, as expected. Also on the porch were: Joy, plus two strollers. Plus Ma.

Plus Harris.

Plus Ryan.

Renee was trotting all awkward up the driveway, trailed by Ryan's mom, pressing a handkerchief to her forehead, and Ryan's dad, bringing up the rear due to a limp I hadn't noticed before.

You! I thought. You jokers? You nutty fuckers are all God sent to stop me? That is a riot. That is so fucking funny. What are you going to stop me with? Your girth? Your good intentions? Your Target jeans? Your years of living off the fat of the land? Your belief that anything and everything can be fixed with talk, talk, endless yapping, hopeful talk?

The contours of the coming disaster expanded to include the deaths of all present.

My face got hot and I thought, Go, go, go.

Ma tried and failed to rise from the porch swing. Ryan helped her up by the elbow all courtly.

Then suddenly something softened in me, maybe at the sight of Ma so weak, and I dropped my head and waded all docile into that crowd of know-nothings, thinking: Okay, okay, you sent me, now bring me back. Find some way to bring me back, you fuckers, or you are the sorriest bunch of bastards the world has ever known.

MY CHIVALRIC FIASCO

Once again it was TorchLightNight.

Around nine I went out to pee. Back in the woods was the big tank that sourced our fake river, plus a pile of old armor.

Don Murray flew past me, looking frazzled. Then I heard a sob. On her back near the armor pile I found Martha from Scullery, peasant skirt up around her waist.

Martha: That guy is my boss. Oh my God oh my God.

I knew Don Murray was her boss because Don Murray was also my boss.

All of a sudden she recognized me.

Ted, don't tell, she said. Please. It's no big deal. Nate can't know. It would kill him.

Then hightailed it out to Parking, eyes black underneath from crying.

Cooking had laid out a big spread on a crude table over by CastleTowerIV: authentic pig heads and whole chickens and blood pudding.

Don Murray stood there moodily picking at some coleslaw.

And gave me the friendliest head shake he'd ever given me.

Women, he said.

See me, said a note on my locker next morning.

In Don Murray's office was Martha.

So Ted, Don Murray said. Last night you witnessed something that, if not viewed in the right light, might seem wrongish. Martha and I find that funny. Don't we, Mar? I just now gave Martha a thousand dollars. In case there was some kind of misunderstanding. Martha now feels we had a fling. Which, both being married, we so much regret. What with the drinking, plus the romance of TorchLightNight, what happened, Martha?

Martha: We got carried away. Had a fling.

Don: Voluntary fling.

Martha: Voluntary fling.

Don: And not only that, Ted. Martha here is moving up. From Scullery. To Floater Thespian. But let's underscore: you are not moving up, Martha, because of our voluntary fling. It's coincidental. Why are you moving up?

Martha: Coincidental.

Don: Coincidental, plus always had a killer work ethic. Ted, you're also moving up. Out of Janitorial. To Pacing Guard.

Which was amazing. I'd been in Janitorial six years. A man of my caliber. That was a joke MQ and I sometimes shared.

Erin would call down and go: MQ, someone threw up in the Grove of Sorrow.

And MQ would be like: A man of my caliber?

Or Erin would go: Ted, some lady dropped her necklace down in the pigpen and is pitching a shit fit.

And I would go: A man of my caliber?

Erin would be like: Get going. It's not funny. She's right up in my grill.

Our pigs were fake and our slop was fake and our poop was fake but still it was no fun to have to don waders and drag the SifterBoyDeLux into the pigpen to, for example, find that lady's necklace. For best results with the SifterBoy-DeLux, you had to first lug the fake pigs off to one side. Being on auto the pigs would continue grunting as you lugged them. Which might look funny if you happened to be holding that particular pig wrong.

Some random guy might go: Look, dude's breast-feeding that pig.

And everyone might laugh.

Therefore a promotion to Pacing Guard was very much welcomed by me.

I was currently the only working person in our family.

Mom being sick, Beth being shy, Dad having sadly cracked his spine recently when a car he was fixing fell on him. We also had some windows that needed replacing. All winter Beth would go around shyly vacuuming up snow. If you came in while she was vacuuming, she would prove too shy to continue.

That night at home Dad calculated we could soon buy Mom a tilting bed.

Dad: If you keep moving up the ladder, maybe in time we can get me a back brace.

Me: Absolutely. I am going to make that happen.

After dinner, driving into town to fill Mom's prescriptions for pain and Beth's prescription for shyness and Dad's prescription for pain, I passed Martha and Nate's.

I honked, did a lean-and-wave, pulled over, got out.

Hey Ted, said Nate.

What's up? I said.

Well, our place sucks, Nate said. Look at this place. Sucks, right? I just can't seem to keep my energy up.

True, their place was pretty bad. The roof was patched with blue sheeting, their kids were doing timid leaps off a wheelbarrow into a mud puddle, a skinny pony was under the swing set licking itself raw like it wanted to be clean when it finally made its break for a nicer living situation.

I mean where are the grown-ups around here? Nate said.

Then he picked a Snotz wrapper off the ground and looked for somewhere to put it. Then dropped it again and it landed on his shoe.

Perfect, he said. Story of my life.

Jeez, Martha said, and plucked it off.

Don't you go south on me too, Nate said. You're all I got, babe.

No I am not, Martha said. You got the kids.

One more thing goes wrong, I'm shooting myself, Nate said.

I kind of doubted he had the get-up-and-go for that. Although you never know.

So what's going on at your guys' work? Nate said. This one here's been super-moody. Even though she just got herself promoted.

I could feel Martha looking at me, like: Ted, I'm in your hands here.

I figured it was her call. Based on my experience of life, which I have not exactly hit out of the park, I tend to agree with that thing about, If it's not broke, don't fix it. And would go even further, to: Even if it is broke, leave it alone, you'll probably make it worse.

So said something about, well, promotions can be hard, they cause a lot of stress.

The gratitude was just beaming off Martha. She walked me back to the car, gave me three tomatoes they'd grown, which, tell the truth, looked kind of geriatric: tiny, timid, wrinkled.

Thank you, she whispered. You saved my life.

———

Next morning in my locker were my Pacing Guard uniform and a Dixie cup with a yellow pill in it.

Hooray, I thought, finally, a Medicated Role.

In came Mrs. Bridges from Health & Safety, with an MSDS on the pill.

Mrs. Bridges: So, this is just going to be a hundred milligrams of KnightLyfe®. To help with the Improv. The thing with KnightLyfe® is, you're going to want to stay hydrated.

I took the pill, went to the Throne Room. I was supposed to Pace in front of a door behind which a King was supposedly thinking. There really was a King in there: Ed Phillips. They put a King in there because one of our Scripted Tropes was: Messenger arrives, charges past Pacing Guard, throws open door, King calls Messenger reckless, calls Pacing Guard a lack-wit, Messenger winces, closes door, has brief exchange with Pacing Guard.

Soon Guests had nearly filled our Fun Spot. The Messenger (a.k.a. Kyle Sperling) barged past me, threw open the door. Ed called Kyle reckless, called me a lackwit. Kyle winced, closed door.

Kyle: I apologize if I have violated protocol.

I blanked on my line, which was: Your rashness bespeaks a manly passion.

Instead I was like: Uh, no problem.

Kyle, a real pro, did not miss a beat.

Kyle (handing me envelope): Please see that he gets this. It is of the utmost urgency.

Me: His Majesty is weighed down with thought.

Kyle: With many burdens of thought?

Me: Right. Many burdens of thought.

Just then the KnightLyfe® kicked in. My mouth went dry. I felt it was nice of Kyle not to give me shit about my mess-up. It occurred to me that I really liked Kyle. Loved him even. Like a brother. A comrade. Noble comrade. I felt we had weathered many storms together. It seemed, for example, that we had, at some point, in some far-distant land, huddled together at the base of a castle wall, hot tar roiling down, and there shared a rueful laugh, as if to say: It is all but brief, so let us live. And then: What ho! Had charged. Up crude ladders, with manly Imprecations, although I could not recall the exact Imprecations, nor the outcome of said Charge.

Kyle departed anon. I did happily entertain our Guests, through use of Wit and various Jibes, glad that I had, after my many Travails, arrived at a station in Life from whence I could impart such Merriment to All & Sundry.

Soon, the Pleasantness of that Day, already Considerable, was much improved by the Arrival of my Benefactor, Don Murray.

Quoth Don Murray, with a gladsome Wink: Ted, you know what you and me should do sometime? Go on a trip or something together. Like a fishing trip? Camping, whatever.

My heart swelled at this Notion. To fish, to hunt, to make Camp with this noble Gentleman! To wander wide Fields & verdant Woods! To rest, at Day's End, in some quiet Bower, beside a coursing Stream, and there, amidst the muted

Whinnying of our Steeds, speak softly of many Things—of Honor; of Love; of Danger; of Duty well-executed!

But then there Occurr'd a fateful Event.

To wit, the Arrival of the aforementioned Martha, in the guise of a Spirit—Spirit Three, to be precise—along with two other Damsels in White (these being Megan and Tiffany). This Trio of Maids did affect a Jolly Ruse: they were Ghosts, who didst Haunt this Castle, with much Shaking of Chain and Sad Laments, as our Guests, in that Fun Spot, confined by the Red Ropes, did Gape & Yaw & Shriek at the Spectacle provided therein.

Glimpsing Martha's Visage—which, though Merry, bore withal a Trace of some Dismal Memory (and I knew well what it was)—I grew, in spite of my recent good Fortune, somewhat Melancholy.

Noting this Change in my Disposition, Martha didst speak to me softly, in an Aside.

Martha: It's cool, Ted. I'm over it. Seriously. I mean it. Drop it.

O, that a Woman of such Enviable Virtue, who had Suffered so, would deign to speak to me in a Manner so Frank & Direct, consenting by her Words to keep her Disgrace in such bleak Confinement!

Martha: Ted. You okay?

To which I made Reply: Verily, I have not been Well, but Distracted & Remiss; but presently am Restored unto Myself, and hereby do make Copious Apology for my earlier Neglect with respect to Thee, dear Lady.

Martha: Easy there, Ted.

At this time, Don Murray himself didst step Forward and, extending his Hand, placed it upon my Breast, as if to Restrain me.

Ted, I swear to God, quoth he. Put a sock in it or I will flush you down the shitter so fast.

And verily, part of my Mind now didst give me sound Counsel: I must endeavor to dampen these Feelings, lest I commit some Rash Act, converting my Good Fortune into Woe.

Yet the Heart of Man is an Organ that doth not offer Itself up to facile Prediction, and shall not be easy Tam'd.

For, as I looked upon Don Murray, many Thoughts did assemble in my Mind, like unto Thunderclouds: Of what Use is Life, if the Living Man doth not pursue Righteousness, & enforce Justice, as God granteth him the Power to do so? Was it a Happy thing, that a Fiend went about Unhindered? Must the Weak forever wander this goodly Orb unprotected? At these Thoughts, something Honest and Manly began to assert itself within me, whereupon, Secrecy not befitting a Gentleman, I strode into the very Center of that Room and sent forth, to the many Guests gathered there, a right Honest Proclamation, in Earnest, & Aloud, to wit:

—That Don Murray had taken Foul Advantage of Martha, placing, against her Will, his Rod into her Womanhood on TorchLightNight;

—Further: that this foul Wretch had Procured Martha's

silence by Various Bribes, including her current Job of Worke;

—Further: that he had similarly attempted to Purchase my Silence; but that I would be SILENT no MORE, for was a Man withal, if nothing ELSE, and would SERVE Righteousness, Regarding NOT the Cost.

Turning to Martha, I requested, by inflection of my Head, her Assent in these Statements, & Confirmation of the Truth of that which I had Declared. But alas! The wench did not Affirm me. Only drop'd her Eyes, as if in Shame, and fled that Place.

Security, being then Summoned by Don Murray, didst arrive and, making much of the Opportunity, had Good Sport of me, delivering many harsh Blows to my Head & Body. And Wrested me from that Place, and Shoved me into the Street, kicking much Dirt upon my Person, and rip'd my Time card to Bits before mine Eyes, and sent it fluttering Aloft, amidst much cruel Laughter at my Expense, especially viz. my Feathered Hat, one Feather of which they had Sore Bent.

I sat, bleeding and bruised, until, summoning what Dignity remained, I made for Home and such Comforts as might be Afforded me there. I had not even Fare to make the Bus (my Backpack having been left behind in that Foul Place), so continued Afoot for well unto an Hour, the Sun by then low in its Arc, all that time Reflecting sadly that, withal, I had Failed in Discrimination, thereby delivering my Family into a most dire Position, whereupon our Poverty, already a Hindrance to our Grace, wouldst be many times Multiplied.

There would be no Back Brace for Father, no Tilting Bed for Mother, and, indeed, the Method by which we would, in future, make Compense for their various Necessary Medicines was now a Mystery, & a Vexation.

Anon I found Myself in proximity of the Wendy's on Center Boulevard, by the closed-down Outback, coming down and coming down hard, aware that, soon, the effect of the Elixir having subsided, I would find myself standing before our iffy Television, struggling to explain, in my own lowly Language, that, tho' Winter's Snows would soon be upon us (entering even unto our Dwelling, as I have earlier Vouchsated), no Appeal wouldst be Brook'd: I was Fired; Fired & sore Disgraced!

Whence came a Death's blow of sorts, underscoring my Folly, delivered by Martha herself, who, calling me upon my Cell Phone, addressed me with true Pain in her Voice, that didst cut me to the Quick, saying: Thanks a million, Ted, in case you didn't notice, we live in a small frigging town, oh my God, oh my God!

At this she began to cry, & in Earnest.

'Twas true: Gossip & Slander did indeed Fly like the Wind in our Town, and would, for sure, reach the Ear of poor dumbfuck Nate soon withal. And finding himself thus cruelly Inform'd of the Foul Violation of his Martha, Nate would definitely freak.

Oh, man.

What a shit Day.

Taking a Shortcut through the high-school practice Field,

where the tackling Dummies, in silhouette, like men who knew the value of holding their Tongues, seemed to Mock at me, I attempted to Comfort myself, saying I had done Right, and served Truth, and shewn good Courage. But 'twas no Comfort in it. It was so weird. Why had I even done That? I felt like a total dickBrain, who should have just left well enough alone, & been more Moderate. I had really screwed the Pooch, no lie. Although, on the other Hand, did not the Devil himself, upon occasion, don the Garb of Moderation, as might befit his Purpose? Was it not Salutary that Events might proceed so as to see Don Murray punish'd? Although, then again, who did I think I was, Mr. Big Shot?

Damn.

Damn it.

What a clusterfuck.

This was going to be Hard to live down.

I was almost completely myself now which, believe me, was no Picnic.

One last bit of Pill got digested by me, seemed like. Producing one last brief but powerful surge of Return. To that former Self. Who, Elevated & Confident to a Fault, had so led me astray.

I took me to the Banks of the River, and tarried there awhile, as the lowering Sun made one with the Water, giving generously of Itself & its Divers Colors, in a Splay of Magnificence that preceded a most wonderful Silence.

TENTH of DECEMBER

The pale boy with unfortunate Prince Valiant bangs and cublike mannerisms hulked to the mudroom closet and requisitioned Dad's white coat. Then requisitioned the boots he'd spray-painted white. Painting the pellet gun white had been a no. That was a gift from Aunt Chloe. Every time she came over he had to haul it out so she could make a big stink about the wood grain.

Today's assignation: walk to pond, ascertain beaver dam. Likely he would be detained. By that species that lived amongst the old rock wall. They were small but, upon emerging, assumed certain proportions. And gave chase. This was just their methodology. His aplomb threw them loops. He knew that. And reveled in it. He would turn, level the pellet gun, intone: Are you aware of the usage of this human implement?

Blam!

They were Netherworlders. Or Nethers. They had a strange bond with him. Sometimes for whole days he would just nurse their wounds. Occasionally, for a joke, he would shoot one in the butt as it fled. Who henceforth would limp for the rest of its days. Which could be as long as an additional nine million years.

Safe inside the rock wall, the shot one would go, Guys, look at my butt.

As a group, all would look at Gzeemon's butt, exchanging sullen glances of: Gzeemon shall indeed be limping for the next nine million years, poor bloke.

Because yes: Nethers tended to talk like that guy in *Mary Poppins*.

Which naturally raised some mysteries as to their ultimate origin here on Earth.

Detaining him was problematic for the Nethers. He was wily. Plus could not fit through their rock-wall opening. When they tied him up and went inside to brew their special miniaturizing potion—*Wham!*— he would snap their antiquated rope with a move from his self-invented martial arts system, Toi Foi, a.k.a., Deadly Forearms. And place at their doorway an implacable rock of suffocation, trapping them inside.

Later, imagining them in their death throes, taking pity on them, he would come back, move the rock.

Blimey, one of them might say from withal. Thanks, guv'nor. You are indeed a worthy adversary.

Sometimes there would be torture. They would make him lie on his back looking up at the racing clouds while they tortured him in ways he could actually take. They tended to leave his teeth alone. Which was lucky. He didn't even like to get a cleaning. They were dunderheads in that manner. They never messed with his peen and never messed with his fingernails. He'd just abide there, infuriating them with his snow angels. Sometimes, believing it their coup de grâce, not realizing he'd heard this since time in memorial from certain in-school cretins, they'd go, Wow, we didn't even know Robin could be a boy's name. And chortle their Nether laughs.

Today he had a feeling that the Nethers might kidnap Suzanne Bledsoe, the new girl in homeroom. She was from Montreal. He just loved the way she talked. So, apparently, did the Nethers, who planned to use her to repopulate their depleted numbers and bake various things they did not know how to bake.

All suited up now, NASA. Turning awkwardly to go out the door.

Affirmative. We have your coordinates. Be careful out there, Robin.

Whoa, cold, dang.

Duck thermometer read ten. And that was without windchill. That made it fun. That made it real. A green Nissan was parked where Poole dead-ended into the soccer field.

Hopefully the owner was not some perv he would have to outwit.

Or a Nether in the human guise.

Bright, bright, blue and cold. Crunch went the snow as he crossed the soccer field. Why did cold such as this give a running guy a headache? Likely it was due to Prominent Windspeed Velocity.

The path into the woods was as wide as one human. It seemed the Nether had indeed kidnapped Suzanne Bledsoe. Damn him! And his ilk. Judging by the single set of tracks, the Nether appeared to be carrying her. Foul cad. He'd better not be touching Suzanne inappropriately while carrying her. If so, Suzanne would no doubt be resisting with untamable fury.

This was concerning, this was very concerning.

When he caught up to them, he would say: Look, Suzanne, I know you don't know my name, having misaddressed me as Roger that time you asked me to scoot over, but nevertheless I must confess I feel there is something to us. Do you feel the same?

Suzanne had the most amazing brown eyes. They were wet now, with fear and sudden reality.

Stop talking to her, mate, the Nether said.

I won't, he said. And Suzanne? Even if you don't feel there is something to us, rest assured I will still slay this fellow and return you home. Where do you live again? Over in El Cirro? By the water tower? Those are some nice houses back there.

Yes, Suzanne said. We also have a pool. You should come

over this summer. It's cool if you swim with your shirt on. And also, yes to there being something to us. You are by far the most insightful boy in our class. Even when I take into consideration the boys I knew in Montreal, I am just like: No one can compare.

Well, that's nice to hear, he said. Thank you for saying that. I know I'm not the thinnest.

The thing about girls? Suzanne said. Is we are more content-driven.

Will you two stop already? the Nether said. Because now is the time for your death. Deaths.

Well, now is certainly the time for somebody's death, Robin said.

The twerpy thing was, you never really got to save anyone. Last summer there'd been a dying raccoon out here. He'd thought of lugging it home so Mom could call the vet. But up close it was too scary. Raccoons being actually bigger than they appear in cartoons. And this one looked like a potential biter. So he ran home to get it some water at least. Upon his return, he saw where the raccoon had done some apparent last-minute thrashing. That was sad. He didn't do well with sad. There had perchance been some pre-weeping, by him, in the woods.

That just means you have a big heart, Suzanne said.

Well, I don't know, he said modestly.

Here was the old truck tire. Where the high-school kids partied. Inside the tire, frosted with snow, were three beer cans and a wadded-up blanket.

You probably like to party, the Nether had cracked to Suzanne moments earlier as they passed this very spot.

No, I don't, Suzanne said. I like to play. And I like to hug.

Hoo boy, the Nether said. Sounds like Dullsville.

Somewhere there is a man who likes to play and hug, Suzanne said.

He came out of the woods now to the prettiest vista he knew. The pond was a pure frozen white. It struck him as somewhat Switzerlandish. Someday he would know for sure. When the Swiss threw him a parade or whatnot.

Here the Nether's tracks departed from the path, as if he had contemplatively taken a moment to gaze at the pond. Perhaps this Nether was not all bad. Perhaps he was having a debilitating conscience-attack vis-à-vis the valiantly struggling Suzanne atop his back. At least he seemed to somewhat love nature.

Then the tracks returned to the path, wound around the pond, and headed up Lexow Hill.

What was this strange object? A coat? On the bench? The bench the Nethers used for their human sacrifices?

No accumulated snow on coat. Inside of coat still slightly warm.

Ergo: the recently discarded coat of the Nether.

This was some strange juju. This was an intriguing conundrum, if he had ever encountered one. Which he had. Once, he'd found a bra on the handlebars of a bike. Once, he'd found an entire untouched steak dinner on a plate behind Fresno's. And hadn't eaten it. Though it had looked pretty good.

Something was afoot.

Then he beheld, halfway up Lexow Hill, a man.

Coatless bald-headed man. Super-skinny. In what looked like pajamas. Climbing plodfully, with tortoise patience, bare white arms sticking out of his p.j. shirt like two bare white branches sticking out of a p.j. shirt. Or grave.

What kind of person leaves his coat behind on a day like this? The mental kind, that was who. This guy looked sort of mental. Like an Auschwitz dude or sad confused grandpa.

Dad had once said, Trust your mind, Rob. If it smells like shit but has writing across it that says Happy Birthday and a candle stuck down in it, what is it?

Is there icing on it? he'd said.

Dad had done that thing of squinting his eyes when an answer was not quite there yet.

What was his mind telling him now?

Something was wrong here. A person needed a coat. Even if the person was a grown-up. The pond was frozen. The duck thermometer said ten. If the person was mental, all the more reason to come to his aid, as had not Jesus said, Blessed are those who help those who cannot help themselves but are too mental, doddering, or have a disability?

He snagged the coat off the bench.

It was a rescue. A real rescue, at last, sort of.

Ten minutes earlier, Don Eber had paused at the pond to catch his breath.

He was so tired. What a thing. Holy moley. When he used to walk Sasquatch out here they'd do six times around the pond, jog up the hill, tag the boulder on top, sprint back down.

Better get moving, said one of two guys who'd been in discussion in his head all morning.

That is, if you're still set on the boulder idea, the other said.

Which still strikes us as kind of fancy-pants.

Seemed like one guy was Dad and the other Kip Flemish.

Stupid cheaters. They'd switched spouses, abandoned the switched spouses, fled together to California. Had they been gay? Or just swingers? Gay swingers? The Dad and Kip in his head had acknowledged their sins and the three of them had struck a deal: he would forgive them for being possible gay swingers and leaving him to do Soap Box Derby alone, with just Mom, and they would consent to giving him some solid manly advice.

He wants it to be nice.

This was Dad now. It seemed Dad was somewhat on his side.

Nice? Kip said. *That is not the word I would use.*

A cardinal zinged across the day.

It was amazing. Amazing, really. He was young. He was fifty-three. Now he'd never deliver his major national speech on compassion. What about going down the Mississippi in a canoe? What about living in an A-frame near a shady creek with the two hippie girls he'd met in 1968 in that souvenir shop in the Ozarks, when Allen, his stepfather, wearing those crazy aviators, had bought him a bag of fossil rocks? One of the hippie girls had said that he, Eber, would be a fox when he grew up, and would he please be sure to call her at that time? Then the hippie girls had put their tawny heads together and giggled at his prospective foxiness. And that had never—

That had somehow never—

Sister Val had said, Why not shoot for being the next JFK? So he had run for class president. Allen had bought him a Styrofoam straw boater. They'd sat together, decorating the hatband with Magic Markers, WIN WITH EBER! On the back: GROOVY! Allen had helped him record a tape. Of a little speech. Allen had taken that tape somewhere and come back with thirty copies, "to pass around."

"Your message is good," Allen had said. "And you are incredibly well spoken. You can do this thing."

And he'd done it. He'd won. Allen had thrown him a victory party. A pizza party. All the kids had come.

Oh, Allen.

Kindest man ever. Had taken him swimming. Had taken him to découpage. Had combed out his hair so patiently that time he came home with lice. Never a harsh, etc., etc.

Not so once the suffering begat. Began. God damn it. More and more his words. Askew. More and more his words were not what he would hoped.

Hope.

Once the suffering began, Allen had raged. Said things no one should say. To Mom, to Eber, to the guy delivering water. Went from a shy man, always placing a reassuring hand on your back, to a diminished pale figure in a bed, shouting CUNT!

Except with some weird New England accent so it came out KANT!

The first time Allen had shouted KANT! there followed a funny moment during which he and Mom looked at each other to see which of them was being called KANT. But then Allen amended, for clarity: KANTS!

So it was clear he meant both of them. What a relief.

They'd cracked up.

Jeez, how long had he been standing here? Daylight was waiting.

Wasting.

I honestly didn't know what to do. But he made it so simple.

Took it all on himself.

So what else is new?

Exactly.

This was Jodi and Tommy now.

Hi, kids.

Big day today.

I mean, sure, it would have been nice to have a chance to say a proper good-bye.

But at what cost?

Exactly. And see—he knew that.

He was a father. That's what a father does.

Eases the burdens of those he loves.

Saves the ones he loves from painful last images that might endure for a lifetime.

Soon Allen had become THAT. And no one was going to fault anybody for avoiding THAT. Sometimes he and Mom would huddle in the kitchen. Rather than risk incurring the wrath of THAT. Even THAT understood the deal. You'd trot in a glass of water, set it down, say, very politely, Anything else, Allen? And you'd see THAT thinking, All these years I was so good to you people and now I am merely THAT? Sometimes the gentle Allen would be inside there too, indicating, with his eyes, Look, go away, please go away, I am trying so hard not to call you KANT!

Rail-thin, ribs sticking out.

Catheter taped to dick.

Waft of shit smell.

You are not Allen and Allen is not you.

So Molly had said.

As for Dr. Spivey, he couldn't say. Wouldn't say. Was busy drawing a daisy on a Post-it. Then finally said, Well, honestly? As these things grow, they can tend to do weird things. But it doesn't necessarily have to be terrible. Had one guy? Just always craved him a Sprite.

And Eber had thought, Did you, dear doctor/savior/lifeline, just say *craved him a Sprite*?

That's how they got you. You thought, Maybe I'll just crave me a Sprite. Next thing you knew, you were THAT, shouting KANT!, shitting your bed, swatting at the people who were scrambling to clean you.

No, sir.

No sirree bob.

Wednesday he'd fallen out of the med bed again. There on the floor in the dark it had come to him: I could spare them.

Spare us? Or spare you?

Get thee behind me.

Get thee behind me, sweetie.

A breeze sent down a sequence of linear snow puffs from somewhere above. Beautiful. Why were we made just so, to find so many things that happened every day pretty?

He took off his coat.

Good Christ.

Took off his hat and gloves, stuffed the hat and gloves in a sleeve of the coat, left the coat on the bench.

This way they'd know. They'd find the car, walk up the path, find the coat.

It was a miracle. That he'd gotten this far. Well, he'd always been strong. Once, he'd run a half-marathon with a broken foot. After his vasectomy he'd cleaned the garage, no problem.

He'd waited in the med bed for Molly to go off to the pharmacy. That was the toughest part. Just calling out a normal good-bye.

His mind veered toward her now, and he jerked it back with a prayer: Let me pull this off. Lord, let me not fuck it up. Let me bring no dishonor. Leg me do it cling.

Let. Let me do it cling.

Clean.

Cleanly.

Estimated time of overtaking the Nether, handing him his coat? Approximately nine minutes. Six minutes to follow the path around the pond, an additional three minutes to fly up the hillside like a delivering wraith or mercy angel, bearing the simple gift of a coat.

That is just an estimate, NASA. I pretty much made that up.

We know that, Robin. We know very well by now how irreverent you work.

Like that time you cut a fart on the moon.

Or the time you tricked Mel into saying, "Mr. President, what a delightful surprise it was to find an asteroid circling Uranus."

That estimate was particularly iffy. This Nether being surprisingly brisk. Robin himself was not the fastest wicket in the stick. He had a certain girth. Which Dad prognosticated would soon triumphantly congeal into linebackerish solidity. He hoped so. For now he just had the slight man boobs.

Robin, hurry, Suzanne said. I feel so sorry for that poor old guy.

He's a fool, Robin said, because Suzanne was young, and did not yet understand that when a man was a fool he made hardships for the other men, who were less foolish than he.

He doesn't have much time, Suzanne said, bordering on the hysterical.

There, there, he said, comforting her.

I'm just so frightened, she said.

And yet he is fortunate to have one such as I to hump his coat up that big-ass hill, which, due to its steepness, is not exactly my cup of tea, Robin said.

I guess that's the definition of "hero," Suzanne said.

I guess so, he said.

I don't mean to continue being insolent, she said. But he seems to be pulling away.

What would you suggest? he said.

With all due respect, she said, and because I know you consider us as equals but different, with me covering the brainy angle and special inventions and whatnot?

Yes, yes, go ahead, he said.

Well, just working through the math in terms of simple geometry—

He saw where she was going with this. And she was quite right. No wonder he loved her. He must cut across the pond, thereby decreasing the ambient angle, ergo trimming valuable seconds off his catch-up time.

Wait, Suzanne said. Is that dangerous?

It is not, he said. I have done it numerous times.

Please be careful, Suzanne implored.

Well, once, he said.

You have such aplomb, Suzanne demurred.

Actually never, he said softly, not wishing to alarm her.

Your bravery is irascible, Suzanne said.

He started across the pond.

It was actually pretty cool walking on water. In summer, canoes floated here. If Mom could see him, she'd have a conniption. Mom treated him like a piece of glass. Due to his alleged infant surgeries. She went on full alert if he so much as used a stapler.

But Mom was a good egg. A reliable counselor and steady hand of guidance. She had a munificent splay of long silver hair and a raspy voice, though she didn't smoke and was even a vegan. She'd never been a biker chick, although some of the in-school cretins claimed she resembled one.

He was actually quite fond of Mom.

He was now approximately three-quarters, or that would be sixty percent, across.

Between him and the shore lay a grayish patch. Here in summer a stream ran in. Looked a tad iffy. At the edge of the grayish patch he gave the ice a bonk with the butt of his gun. Solid as anything.

Here he went. Ice rolled a bit underfoot. Probably it was shallow here. Anyways he hoped so. Yikes.

How's it going? Suzanne said, trepidly.

Could be better, he said.

Maybe you should turn back, Suzanne said.

But wasn't this feeling of fear the exact feeling all heroes had to confront early in life? Wasn't overcoming this feeling of fear what truly distinguished the brave?

There could be no turning back.

Or could there? Maybe there could. Actually there should.

The ice gave way and the boy fell through.

Nausea had not been mentioned in *The Humbling Steppe*.

A blissful feeling overtook me as I drifted off to sleep at the base of the crevasse. No fear, no discomfort, only a vague sadness at the thought of all that remained undone. This is death? I thought. It is but nothing.

Author, whose name I cannot remember, I would like a word with you.

A-hole.

The shivering was insane. Like a tremor. His head was shaking on his neck. He paused to puke a bit in the snow, white-yellow against the white-blue.

This was scary. This was scary now.

Every step was a victory. He had to remember that. With every step he was fleeing father and father. Farther from father. Stepfarther. What a victory he was wresting. From the jaws of the feet.

He felt a need at the back of his throat to say it right.

From the jaws of defeat. From the jaws of defeat.

Oh, Allen.

Even when you were THAT you were still Allen to me.

Please know that.

Falling, Dad said.

For some definite time he waited to see where he would

land and how much it would hurt. Then there was a tree in his gut. He found himself wrapped fetally around some tree. Fucksake.

Ouch, ouch. This was too much. He hadn't cried after the surgeries or during the chemo, but he felt like crying now. It wasn't fair. It happened to everyone supposedly but now it was happening specifically to him. He'd kept waiting for some special dispensation. But no. Something/someone bigger than him kept refusing. You were told the big something/someone loved you especially but in the end you saw it was otherwise. The big something/someone was neutral. Unconcerned. When it innocently moved, it crushed people.

Years ago at *The Illuminated Body* he and Molly had seen this brain slice. Marring the brain slice had been a nickel-sized brown spot. That brown spot was all it had taken to kill the guy. Guy must have had his hopes and dreams, closet full of pants, and so on, some treasured childhood memories: a mob of koi in the willow shade at Gage Park, say, Gram searching in her Wrigley's-smelling purse for a tissue—like that. If not for that brown spot, the guy might have been one of the people walking by on the way to lunch in the atrium. But no. He was defunct now, off rotting somewhere, no brain in his head.

Looking down at the brain slice Eber had felt a sense of superiority. Poor guy. It was pretty unlucky, what had happened to him.

He and Molly had fled to the atrium, had hot scones, watched a squirrel mess with a plastic cup.

Wrapped fetally around the tree Eber traced the scar on his head. Tried to sit. No dice. Tried to use the tree to sit up. His hand wouldn't close. Reaching around the tree with both hands, joining his hands at the wrists, he pulled himself up, leaned back against the tree.

How was that?

Fine.

Good, actually.

Maybe this was it. Maybe this was as far as he got. He'd had it in mind to sit cross-legged against the boulder at the top of the hill, but really what difference did it make?

All he had to do now was stay put. Stay put by force-thinking the same thoughts he'd used to propel himself out of the med bed and into the car and across the soccer field and through the woods: MollyTommyJodi huddling in the kitchen filled with pity/loathing, MollyTommyJodi recoiling at something cruel he'd said, Tommy hefting his thin torso up in his arms so that MollyJodi could get under there with a wash—

Then it would be done. He would have preempted all future debasement. All his fears about the coming months would be mute.

Moot.

This was it. Was it? Not yet. Soon, though. An hour? Forty minutes? Was he doing this? Really? He was. Was he? Would he be able to make it back to the car even if he changed his mind? He thought not. Here he was. He was here. This incredible opportunity to end things with dignity was right in his hands.

All he had to do was stay put.

I will fight no more forever.

Concentrate on the beauty of the pond, the beauty of the woods, the beauty you are returning to, the beauty that is everywhere as far as you can—

Oh, for shitsake.

Oh, for crying out loud.

Some kid was on the pond.

Chubby kid in white. With a gun. Carrying Eber's coat.

You little fart, put that coat down, get your ass home, mind your own—

Damn. Damn it.

Kid tapped the ice with the butt of his gun.

You wouldn't want some kid finding you. That could scar a kid. Although kids found freaky things all the time. Once he'd found a naked photo of Dad and Mrs. Flemish. That had been freaky. Of course, not as freaky as a grimacing cross-legged—

Kid was swimming.

Swimming was not allowed. That was clearly posted. NO SWIMMING.

Kid was a bad swimmer. Real thrashfest down there. Kid was creating with his thrashing a rapidly expanding black pool. With each thrash the kid incrementally expanded the boundary of the black—

He was on his way down before he knew he'd started. *Kid in the pond, kid in the pond,* ran repetitively through his head as he minced. Progress was tree to tree. Standing there panting, you got to know a tree well. This one had three knots: eye, eye, nose. This started out as one tree and became two.

Suddenly he was not purely the dying guy who woke nights in the med bed thinking, Make this not true make this not true, but again, partly, the guy who used to put bananas in the freezer, then crack them on the counter and pour chocolate over the broken chunks, the guy who'd once stood outside a classroom window in a rainstorm to see how Jodi was faring with that little red-headed shit who wouldn't give her a chance at the book table, the guy who used to hand-paint birdfeeders in college and sell them on weekends in Boulder, wearing a jester hat and doing a little juggling routine he'd—

He started to fall again, caught himself, froze in a hunched-over position, hurtled forward, fell flat on his face, chucked his chin on a root.

You had to laugh.

You almost had to laugh.

He got up. Got doggedly up. His right hand presented as a bloody glove. Tough nuts, too bad. Once, in football, a tooth had come out. Later in the half, Eddie Blandik had found it. He'd taken it from Eddie, flung it away. That had also been him.

Here was the switchbank. It wasn't far now. Switchback.

What to do? When he got there? Get kid out of pond. Get kid moving. Force-walk kid through woods, across soccer field, to one of the houses on Poole. If nobody home, pile kid into Nissan, crank up heater, drive to—Our Lady of Sorrows? UrgentCare? Fastest route to UrgentCare?

Fifty yards to the trailhead.

Twenty yards to the trailhead.

Thank you, God, for my strength.

In the pond he was all animal-thought, no words, no self, blind panic. He resolved to really try. He grabbed for the edge. The edge broke away. Down he went. He hit mud and pushed up. He grabbed for the edge. The edge broke away. Down he went. It seemed like it should be easy, getting out. But he just couldn't do it. It was like at the carnival. It should be easy to knock three sawdust dogs off a ledge. And it was easy. It just wasn't easy with the amount of balls they gave you.

He wanted the shore. He knew that was the right place for him. But the pond kept saying no.

Then it said maybe.

The ice edge broke again, but, breaking it, he pulled himself infinitesimally toward shore, so that, when he went down, his feet found mud sooner. The bank was sloped. Suddenly there was hope. He went nuts. He went total spaz. Then he was out, water streaming off him, a piece of ice like a tiny pane of glass in the cuff of his coat.

Trapezoidal, he thought.

In his mind, the pond was not finite, circular, and behind him but infinite and all around.

He felt he'd better lie still or whatever had just tried to kill him would try again. What had tried to kill him was not just in the pond but out here, too, in every natural thing, and there was no him, no Suzanne, no Mom, no nothing, just the sound of some kid crying like a terrified baby.

Eber jog-hobbled out of the woods and found: no kid. Just black water. And a green coat. His coat. His former coat, out there on the ice. The water was calming already.

Oh, shit.

Your fault.

Kid was only out there because of—

Down on the beach near an overturned boat was some ignoramus. Lying facedown. On the job. Lying down on the job. Must have been lying there even as that poor kid—

Wait, rewind.

It was the kid. Oh, thank Christ. Facedown like a corpse in a Brady photo. Legs still in the pond. Like he'd lost steam crawling out. Kid was soaked through, the white coat gone gray with wet.

Eber dragged the kid out. It took four distinct pulls. He didn't have the strength to flip him over, but, turning the head, at least got the mouth out of the snow.

Kid was in trouble.

Soaking wet, ten degrees.

Doom.

Eber went down on one knee and told the kid in a grave fatherly way that he had to get up, had to get moving or he could lose his legs, he could die.

The kid looked at Eber, blinked, stayed where he was.

He grabbed the kid by the coat, rolled him over, roughly sat him up. The kid's shivers made his shivers look like nothing. Kid seemed to be holding a jackhammer. He had to get the kid warmed up. How to do it? Hug him, lie on top of him? That would be like Popsicle-on-Popsicle.

Eber remembered his coat, out on the ice, at the edge of the black water.

Ugh.

Find a branch. No branches anywhere. Where the heck was a good fallen branch when you—

All right, all right, he'd do it without a branch.

He walked fifty feet downshore, stepped onto the pond, walked a wide loop on the solid stuff, turned to shore, started toward the black water. His knees were shaking. Why? He was afraid he might fall in. Ha. Dope. Poser. The coat was fifteen feet away. His legs were in revolt. His legs were revolting.

Doctor, my legs are revolting.

You're telling me.

He tiny-stepped up. The coat was ten feet away. He went

down on his knees, knee-walked slightly up. Went down on his belly. Stretched out an arm.

Slid forward on his belly.

Bit more.

Bit more.

Then had a tiny corner by two fingers. He hauled it in, slid himself back via something like a reverse breaststroke, got to his knees, stood, retreated a few steps, and was once again fifteen feet away and safe.

Then it was like the old days, getting Tommy or Jodi ready for bed when they were zonked. You said, "Arm," the kid lifted an arm. You said, "Other arm," the kid lifted the other arm. With the coat off, Eber could see that the boy's shirt was turning to ice. Eber peeled the shirt off. Poor little guy. A person was just some meat on a frame. Little guy wouldn't last long in this cold. Eber took off his pajama shirt, put it on the kid, slid the kid's arm into the arm of the coat. In the arm was Eber's hat and gloves. He put the hat and gloves on the kid, zipped the coat up.

The kid's pants were frozen solid. His boots were ice sculptures of boots.

You had to do things right. Eber sat on the boat, took off his boots and socks, peeled off his pajama pants, made the kid sit on the boat, knelt before the kid, got the kid's boots off. He loosened the pants up with little punches and soon had one leg partly out. He was stripping off a kid in ten-degree weather. Maybe this was exactly the wrong thing. Maybe he'd kill the kid. He didn't know. He just didn't know. Desperately, he gave the pants a few more punches. Then the kid was stepping out.

Eber put the pajama pants on him, then the socks, then the boots.

The kid was standing there in Eber's clothes, swaying, eyes closed.

We're going to walk now, okay? Eber said.

Nothing.

Eber gave the kid an encouraging pop in the shoulders. Like a football thing.

We're going to walk you home, he said. Do you live near here?

Nothing.

He gave a harder pop.

The kid gaped at him, baffled.

Pop.

Kid started walking.

Pop-pop.

Like fleeing.

Eber drove the kid out ahead of him. Like cowboy and cow. At first, fear of the popping seemed to be motivating the kid, but then good old panic kicked in and he started running. Soon Eber couldn't keep up.

Kid was at the bench. Kid was at the trailhead.

Good boy, get home.

Kid disappeared into the woods.

Eber came back to himself.

Oh, boy. Oh, wow.

He had never known cold. Had never known tired.

He was standing in the snow in his underwear near an overturned boat.

He hobbled to the boat and sat in the snow.

Robin ran.

Past the bench and the trailhead and into the woods on the old familiar path.

What the heck? What the heck had just happened? He'd fallen into the pond? His jeans had frozen solid? Had ceased being blue jeans. Were white jeans. He looked down to see if his jeans were still white jeans.

He had on pajama pants that, tucked into some tremendoid boots, looked like clown pants.

Had he been crying just now?

I think crying is healthy, Suzanne said. It means you're in touch with your feelings.

Ugh. That was done, that was stupid, talking in your head to some girl who in real life called you Roger.

Dang.

So tired.

Here was a stump.

He sat. It felt good to rest. He wasn't going to lose his legs. They didn't even hurt. He couldn't even feel them. He wasn't going to die. Dying was not something he had in mind at this early an age. To rest more efficiently, he lay down. The sky was blue. The pines swayed. Not all at the same rate. He raised one gloved hand and watched it tremor.

He might close his eyes for a bit. Sometimes in life one felt a feeling of wanting to quit. Then everyone would see. Everyone would see that teasing wasn't nice. Sometimes with all the teasing his days were subtenable. Sometimes he felt he couldn't take even one more lunchtime of meekly eating on that rolled-up wrestling mat in the cafeteria corner near the snapped parallel bars. He did not have to sit there. But preferred to. If he sat anywhere else, there was the chance of a comment or two. Upon which he would then have the rest of the day to reflect. Sometimes comments were made on the clutter of his home. Thanks to Bryce, who had once come over. Sometimes comments were made on his manner of speaking. Sometimes comments were made on the style faux pas of Mom. Who was, it must be said, a real eighties gal.

Mom.

He did not like it when they teased about Mom. Mom had no idea of his lowly school status. Mom seeing him more as the paragon or golden-boy type.

Once, he'd done a secret rendezvous of recording Mom's phone calls, just for the reconnaissance aspect. Mostly they were dull, mundane, not about him at all.

Except for this one with her friend Liz.

I never dreamed I could love someone so much, Mom had said. I just worry I might not be able to live up to him, you know? He's so *good,* so *grateful.* That kid deserves—that kid deserves it all. Better school, which we cannot afford, some trips, like abroad, but that is also, uh, out of our price range. I just don't want to *fail* him, you know? That's all I want from my life, you know? Liz? To feel, at the end, like I did right by that magnificent little dude.

At that point it seemed like Liz had maybe started vacuuming.

Magnificent little dude.

He should probably get going.

Magnificent Little Dude was like his Indian name.

He got to his feet and, gathering his massive amount of clothes up like some sort of encumbering royal train, started toward home.

Here was the truck tire, here the place where the trail briefly widened, here the place where the trees crossed overhead like reaching for one another. Weave ceiling, Mom called it.

Here was the soccer field. Across the field, his house sat like a big sweet animal. It was amazing. He'd made it. He'd fallen into the pond and lived to tell the tale. He had somewhat cried, yes, but had then simply laughed off this moment of mortal weakness and made his way home, look of wry bemusement on his face, having, it must be acknowledged, benefited from the much appreciated assistance of a certain aged—

With a shock he remembered the old guy. What the heck? An image flashed of the old guy standing bereft and blue-skinned in his tighty-whities like a P.O.W. abandoned at the

barbed wire due to no room on the truck. Or a sad trauma-
tized stork bidding farewell to its young.

He'd bolted. He'd bolted on the old guy. Hadn't even
given him a thought.

Blimey.

What a chickenshitish thing to do.

He had to go back. Right now. Help the old guy hobble
out. But he was so tired. He wasn't sure he could do it. Probably the old guy was fine. Probably he had some sort of
old-guy plan.

But he'd bolted. He couldn't live with that. His mind was
telling him that the only way to undo the bolting was to go
back now, save the day. His body was saying something else:
It's too far, you're just a kid, get Mom, Mom will know what
to do.

He stood paralyzed at the edge of the soccer field like a
scarecrow in huge flowing clothes.

Eber sat slumped against the boat.

What a change in the weather. People were going around
with parasols and so forth in the open part of the park.
There was a merry-go-round and a band and a gazebo. People were frying food on the backs of certain merry-go-round
horses. And yet, on others, kids were riding. How did they
know? Which horses were hot? For now there was still snow,
but snow couldn't last long in this bomb.

Balm.

If you close your eyes, that's the end. You know that, right?

Hilarious.

Allen.

His exact voice. After all these years.

Where was he? The duck pond. So many times he'd come out here with the kids. He should go now. Good-bye, duck pond. Although hang on. He couldn't seem to stand. Plus you couldn't leave a couple of little kids behind. Not this close to water. They were four and six. For God's sake. What had he been thinking? Leaving those two little dears by the pond. They were good kids, they'd wait, but wouldn't they get bored? And swim? Without life jackets? No, no, no. It made him sick. He had to stay. Poor kids. Poor abandoned—

Wait, rewind.

His kids were excellent swimmers.

His kids had never come close to being abandoned.

His kids were grown.

Tom was thirty. Tall drink of water. Tried so hard to know things. But even when he thought he knew a thing (fighting kites, breeding rabbits), Tom would soon be shown for what he was: the dearest, most agreeable young fellow ever, who knew no more about fighting kites/breeding rabbits than the average person could pick up from ten minutes on the Internet. Not that Tom wasn't smart. Tom was smart. Tom was a damn quick study. O Tom, Tommy, Tommikins! The heart in that kid! He just worked and worked. For the love of his dad. Oh, kid, you had it, you have it, Tom,

Tommy, even now I am thinking of you, you are very much on my mind.

And Jodi, Jodi was out there in Santa Fe. She'd said she'd take off work and fly home. As needed. But there was no need. He didn't like to impose. The kids had their own lives. Jodi-Jode. Little freckle-face. Pregnant now. Not married. Not even dating. Stupid Lars. What kind of man deserted a beautiful girl like that? A total dear. Just starting to make some progress in her job. You couldn't take that kind of time off when you'd only just started—

Reconstructing the kids in this way was having the effect of making them real to him again. Which—you didn't want to get that ball roiling. Jodi was having a baby. Rolling. He could have lasted long enough to see the baby. Hold the baby. It was sad, yes. That was a sacrifice he'd had to make. He'd explained it in the note. Hadn't he? No. Hadn't left a note. Couldn't. There'd been some reason he couldn't. Hadn't there? He was pretty sure there'd been some—

Insurance. It couldn't seem like he'd done it on purpose.

Little panic.

Little panic here.

He was offing himself. Offing himself, he'd involved a kid. Who was wandering the woods hypothermic. Offing himself two weeks before Christmas. Molly's favorite holiday. Molly had a valve thing, a panic thing, this business might—

This was not—this was not him. This was not something he would have done. Not something he would ever do. Except he—he'd done it. He was doing it. It was in progress. If he didn't get moving, it would—it would be accomplished. It would be done.

This very day you will be with me in the kingdom of—
He had to fight.

But couldn't seem to keep his eyes open.

He tried to send some last thoughts to Molly. Sweetie, forgive me. Biggest fuckup ever. Forget this part. Forget I ended thisly. You know me. You know I didn't mean this.

He was at his house. He wasn't at his house. He knew that. But could see every detail. Here was the empty med bed, the studio portrait of HimMollyTommyJodi posed around that fake rodeo fence. Here was the little bedside table. His meds in the pillbox. The bell he rang to call Molly. What a thing. What a cruel thing. Suddenly he saw clearly how cruel it was. And selfish. Oh, God. Who was he? The front door swung open. Molly called his name. He'd hide in the sunroom. Jump out, surprise her. Somehow they'd remodeled. Their sunroom was now the sunroom of Mrs. Kendall, his childhood piano teacher. That would be fun for the kids, to take piano lessons in the same room where he'd—

Hello? said Mrs. Kendall.

What she meant was: Don't die yet. There are many of us who wish to judge you harshly in the sunroom.

Hello, hello! she shouted.

Coming around the pond was a silver-haired woman.

All he had to do was call out.

He called out.

To keep him alive she started piling on him various things from life, things smelling of a home—coats, sweaters, a rain of flowers, a hat, socks, sneakers—and with amazing strength had him on his feet and was maneuvering him into a maze of trees, a wonderland of trees, trees hung with ice. He was piled high with clothes. He was like the bed at a party on which they pile the coats. She had all the answers: where to step, when to rest. She was strong as a bull. He was on her hip now like a baby; she had both arms around his waist, lifting him over a root.

They walked for hours, seemed like. She sang. Cajoled. She hissed at him, reminding him, with pokes in the forehead (right in his forehead) that her freaking *kid* was at *home*, near *frozen*, so they had to *book it*.

Good God, there was so much to do. If he made it. He'd make it. This gal wouldn't let him not make it. He'd have to try to get Molly to see—see why he'd done it. *I was scared, I was scared, Mol.* Maybe Molly would agree not to tell Tommy and Jodi. He didn't like the thought of them knowing he'd been scared. Didn't like the thought of them knowing what a fool he'd been. Oh, to hell with that! Tell everyone! He'd done it! He'd been driven to do it and he'd done it and that was it. That was him. That was part of who he was. No more lies, no more silence, it was going to be a new and different life, if only he—

They were crossing the soccer field.

Here was the Nissan.

His first thought was: Get in, drive it home.

Oh, no, you don't, she said with that smoky laugh and guided him into a house. A house on the park. He'd seen it a million times. And now was in it. It smelled of man sweat and spaghetti sauce and old books. Like a library where sweaty men went to cook spaghetti. She sat him in front of a woodstove, brought him a brown blanket that smelled of medicine. Didn't talk but in directives: Drink this, let me take that, wrap up, what's your name, what's your number?

What a thing! To go from dying in your underwear in the snow to this! Warmth, colors, antlers on the walls, an old-time crank phone like you saw in silent movies. It was something. Every second was something. He hadn't died in his shorts by a pond in the snow. The kid wasn't dead. He'd killed no one. Ha! Somehow he'd got it all back. Everything was good now, everything was—

The woman reached down, touched his scar.

Oh, wow, ouch, she said. You didn't do that out there, did you?

At this he remembered that the brown spot was as much in his head as ever.

Oh, Lord, there was still all that to go through.

Did he still want it? Did he still want to live?

Yes, yes, oh, God, yes, please.

Because, okay, the thing was—he saw it now, was starting to see it—if some guy, at the end, fell apart, and said or did bad things, or had to be helped, helped to quite a considerable extent? So what? What of it? Why should he not do or say weird things or look strange or disgusting? Why should the shit not run down his legs? Why should those he loved not lift and bend and feed and wipe him, when he would gladly do the same for them? He'd been afraid to be lessened by the lifting and bending and feeding and wiping, and was still afraid of that, and yet, at the same time, now saw that there could still be many—many drops of goodness, is how it came to him—many drops of happy—of good fellowship—ahead, and those drops of fellowship were not—had never been—his to withheld.

Withhold.

The kid came out of the kitchen, lost in Eber's big coat, pajama pants pooling around his feet with the boots now off. He took Eber's bloody hand gently. Said he was sorry. Sorry for being such a dope in the woods. Sorry for running off. He'd just been out of it. Kind of scared and all.

Listen, Eber said hoarsely. You did amazing. You did perfect. I'm here. Who did that?

There. That was something you could do. The kid maybe felt better now? He'd given the kid that? That was a reason. To stay around. Wasn't it? Can't console anyone if not around? Can't do squat if gone?

When Allen was close to the end, Eber had done a presentation at school on the manatee. Got an A from Sister Eustace. Who could be quite tough. She was missing two fingers on her right hand from a lawn-mower incident and sometimes used that hand to scare a kid silent.

He hadn't thought of this in years.

She'd put that hand on his shoulder not to scare him but as a form of praise. *That was just terrific. Everyone should take their work as seriously as Donald here. Donald, I hope you'll go home and share this with your parents.* He'd gone home and shared it with Mom. Who'd suggested he share it with Allen. Who, on that day, had been more Allen than THAT. And Allen—

Ha, wow, Allen. There was a man.

Tears sprang into his eyes as he sat by the woodstove.

Allen had—Allen had said it was great. Asked a few questions. About the manatee. What did they eat again? Did he think they could effectively communicate with one another? What a trial that must have been! In his condition. Forty minutes on the manatee? Including a poem Eber had composed? A sonnet? On the manatee?

He'd felt so happy to have Allen back.

I'll be like him, he thought. I'll try to be like him.

The voice in his head was shaky, hollow, unconvinced.

Then: sirens.

Somehow: Molly.

He heard her in the entryway. Mol, Molly, oh boy. When they were first married they used to fight. Say the most insane things. Afterward, sometimes there would be tears. Tears in bed? And then they would—Molly pressing her hot wet face against his hot wet face. They were sorry, they were saying with their bodies, they were accepting each other back, and that feeling, that feeling of being accepted back again and again, of someone's affection for you expanding

to encompass whatever new flawed thing had just mani-
fested in you, that was the deepest, dearest thing he'd ever—

She came in flustered and apologetic, a touch of anger in
her face. He'd embarrassed her. He saw that. He'd embarrassed her by doing something that showed she hadn't suffi-
ciently noticed him needing her. She'd been too busy nursing
him to notice how scared he was. She was angry at him for
pulling this stunt and ashamed of herself for feeling angry at
him in his hour of need, and was trying to put the shame and
anger behind her now so she could do what might be needed.

All of this was in her face. He knew her so well.

Also concern.

Overriding everything else in that lovely face was concern.

She came to him now, stumbling a bit on a swell in the
floor of this stranger's house.

ACKNOWLEDGMENTS

I would like to thank the MacArthur Foundation, the Guggenheim Foundation, the American Academy of Arts and Letters, and Syracuse University for their generous support during the writing of this book.

I would also like to thank:

Esther Newberg, for her tireless guidance and friendship these last sixteen years, during which she has given me the great gift of making me feel that all I had to do was write as well as I could, and she would take care of the rest, which she has, with incredible discernment and energy.

Deborah Treisman, for the masterful editing she does on my work for *The New Yorker,* the generous and gracious way in which she does it, and the expansive effect her opinions always have on my work.

Andy Ward, for his friendship, wise counsel, and faith in me, and for the happy influence of his constantly positive outlook—in Dubai, Nepal, Africa, Mexico, Fresno, and as we worked together on this book.

Caitlin and Alena: watching you all these years has taught me that goodness is not only possible, it is our natural state.

Paula: everything worthwhile I've done over the past twenty-five years has been inspired, selflessly supported, and lovingly informed by your kindness, your advice, and your undying faith. Thank you one million times. Somewhere in my youth or childhood, I must have done something really freaking good.

ABOUT THE AUTHOR

George Saunders is the author of six previous books, including the story collections *CivilWar-Land in Bad Decline, Pastoralia,* and *In Persuasion Nation.* He has received fellowships from the Lannan Foundation, the American Academy of Arts and Letters, and the Guggenheim Foundation. In 2006 he was awarded a MacArthur Fellowship. He teaches in the Creative Writing Program at Syracuse University.

ABOUT THE TYPE

This book was set in Sabon, a typeface designed by the well-known German typographer Jan Tschichold (1902–74). Sabon's design is based upon the original letter forms of Claude Garamond and was created specifically to be used for three sources: foundry type for hand composition, Linotype, and Monotype. Tschichold named his typeface for the famous Frankfurt typefounder Jacques Sabon, who died in 1580.